# *The* STICKY PLACE

## *between*

# HOPE *and* HEARTBREAK

A Short Story Collection

*I hope you will Be blessed by some of these stories. Enjoy! Sept 3:17*

## Rachel Friday

*Rachel Friday*

To Mom who has always believed in me.

To my husband, Ravi,
who said I could do it.

To Sangeeta, Jesse, Jamie, and Nina
who put up with me reading these stories out
loud afterschool and still love me.

# Acknowledgements

A ginormous, heartfelt thank you to my editing friends: Linda, Jenn, Evelyn, Amy, Shenandoah, Dulce, Sharmee, Stephanie, Tara, Sophia, Lena, and the whole Sand Creek Gang: Shannon, Logan, Nigel, Dan, Mike, Susan and the others who have dropped by.

—R.F.

# Table of Contents

# First Kiss

One of us needs to be slapped back into reality, and I'm almost sure it's not him. I feel stupid standing here, squeezing this borrowed satin clutch with both hands as if my life depended on it. I don't know whether to run to him or run away.

My body is so numb, I no longer feel the flimsy material I draped over it earlier today. Maybe it's because my heart's cards are all laid on the table, or maybe it's because my dress has fallen to the floor or been burned away by the heat emanating from within.

His face conveys nothing of my own staggering fear, suffocating guilt, and reckless desire brewing together right below the surface. I feel like one of those rich, bimbo, wannabe heroines from my older sister's romance collection when I was a kid. Sneaking into the bathroom at age eleven to read about the perky, white bosoms throbbing against the man's hard, hairless chest…blah, blah, blah. *Then* I felt like giggling. *Now* I feel like throwing up.

You would think I'd never been kissed before, never been touched before. Mercy! I've been loved, touched, and made love to by my precious husband for umpteen years with more than my share of sweet and spicy kisses.

But today is a new day and this is not my husband.

Boldness lights up his face as this man stands before me. His eyes invite me to step closer, but I am rooted in place. I'm not sure I want anything to do with what's going on between us right now—after all, he does not belong to me. That is the part I cannot forget. My mind is signaling "Mayday! Mayday!" but my body has a mind of its own.

The hair above his ears has grayed in waves, accenting the laugh lines at the corners of his eyes. His smile, nervous and genuine, seems to be asking more than, "Can I hold your hand?" The heat, which fills the flimsy six feet between us, speaks with a more earnest voice. We may be more mature, but having him this close makes me feel like a teenager at her first dance.

On the other hand, it's not unpleasant. Part of me wants to run to him—or better yet, have him come over here next to me, right now. My chest feels still and full, like my heart is holding its breath. What if I let this man take a few steps closer? Once we kiss, my life will never be the same.

Suddenly the setting sun in the window behind him, the chattering laughter of passersby outside, his breathing, and my breathing—everything slows down as I remember a first kiss from long ago.

*Nine years old and scrappy in overalls, my tangle of dirt-colored hair has not been combed since yesterday. Barefoot all summer, I play with the neighbor's kids in the cow pasture behind Granddaddy's house. The early dew is nearly gone, and the air is thick with heat. We chase the cows, the butterflies, and one another. We spit watermelon seeds, pick blackberries, and tell jokes. I make a crown of white clover and place it on my head. Becca is somewhere behind me, laughing at something her brother just said. I look up to see what it's all about.*

*A few feet away, a cow flaps her tail at a biting fly, and some June-bugs join our play. Becca's twelve-year-old brother sees me in my flower crown, and he raises his eyebrows, like he's surprised to find a queen in a field of weeds so early in the morning. The silliness of the boy drops away for a moment, and with a blur of freckles, a quick, soft impression is made on my cheek.*

*I am surprised, too, and for a second I recognize the pleasure of the thing. Then he snatches the crown off my head, pulling my hair along with it, and runs toward an unsuspecting cow, with what she might deem sinister intentions. As the ornery in the boy resurfaces, the magic of the memory fades from my mind's eye.*

It is a strange sensation when you are about to give in to something like this. My body is rigid, my mind alert. Something within me is pulsing, vibrating, humming—like a rodeo horse behind the gate, huffing, pawing, and ready to burst out from his skin when the gate is thrown. If I could harness the intensity coursing through me, I could hike up and down the fourteen stories below me, several times, without weakening. Or maybe I could get my whole house clean in one swoop. That's what I *should* be doing right now, instead of standing here like a statue. It's not the first time in my life to feel so befuddled.

*Seventh grade and awkward, wondering what it's like to be somebody's princess, I have acted like a fool to get the attention of a tall, pimple-faced boy in my homeroom. Two rows away with my stringy hair, breasts in training, and ill-fitting clothes—could he be fooled into thinking I am somebody special?*

*If only I could exude confidence and beauty while I sit reading. I try to appear sophisticated and lust-worthy, like any of the popular girls with their self-assured smiles and burgeoning curves. My legs are crossed, my back is swayed,* and my hand is clutching a paperback. I try to look demure and tempting—tempting for what, I have no idea.

Eliciting no response, I turn towards him, cock my head to one side, and twist the hair behind my right ear with one long, pretty finger. He is still fully engaged with the Hardy Boys!

I wiggle, sigh, and try every kind of pose imaginable that might send him vibes of my alluring personality and vibrant femininity. When twenty minutes of assigned reading are over, I pick up my book bag and slump toward the lockers. He sidles up behind me in the hallway and nudges my shoulder. "Hey, girl."

I turn to look up into his face with my most winning smile, and he sneers, "You got ants in your pants or what?"

I could just die. My cheeks burn crimson, as I stumble through the crowded hallway to the band room.

From then on, I avoid his eyes, his locker, and his route through the halls. Two days later, behind the school, his impertinent face looms in. His lips are salty with sweat as they press against my own. One second I am alone, walking toward the busses under the weight of my backpack and the next his fishy tongue is poking at my mouth.

Stunned, I blink at him. Then he makes his explanation, but it's not for me.

*"Told you she'd let me," he says, and now I see three other boys, yucky and hateful with their sneers and filthy comments. With my eyes lowered to the ground, I storm off to the bus.*

He's still looking at me. He may have been talking to me, but I have been lost in memory. He is not my husband and I think that's what stirs up the most fear. But I am also excited. Who is this man to be in my life? What will this become? How should I act? What will people think? Women like *me* don't feel like *this* so late in life. Maybe it's better to stick with what is familiar, routine, and proper. In my frustration, long-suppressed curse words come to mind, words in a language not my own. I am remembering a club I visited once upon a time in college.

*Nineteen and unsophisticated, I am on an exchange program in Germany. The half-dressed and half-drunk, coarser-behaving girls giggle, curse, and smoke the night away in some kind of club. I don't know why I'm here with this crowd of strangers. I don't understand most of what is going on around me, except that a nice guy sits across from me. I can tell he is like me—too straight-laced to be in a place like this.*

*With boundaries of respectability as comfortable to him as a well-worn pair of shoes, he grabs his Coke in one hand, mine in the other, and we slide out of the booth. Loud music thumps within my chest as I edge toward the door. I manage to squeeze out from among the gyrating people without losing my head, my virginity, or even my shoes.*

*Out on the sidewalk the man holds the Coke out to me and smiles. I mouth "danke" and take a long, slow drink. Outside there's less noise and less cigarette smoke. With my broken German and his crippled English, we talk and laugh and thoroughly enjoy one another till the wee hours.*

*He walks me back to my apartment just as the sun yawns and stretches over the horizon. Shyly, we say our good-byes, neither one of us wanting our time together to end. He leans in, pausing as if to ask permission. Then seeing my smiling eyes, his lips caress mine tenderly and respectfully. All at once, his back is to me, and I never see him again.*

At ages twenty-nine, thirty-five, forty-two, and fifty—I have had many kisses—fervent and significant, conveying regret and delight, forgiveness and gratitude. Most were with my husband. Many have been forgotten.

The man I am with now steps toward me and takes my face in his hands. A shudder of excitement threatens to topple my composure. On the verge of another first kiss—with another man, can it be alright?

Spotted and wrinkled at eighty-seven and widowed for thirteen years, I am still scrappy, awkward, and unsophisticated. I have long since gotten over the shyness, the need to please, and the insecurity that hovers over the young. I have known what it is to be someone special, loved, appreciated, and enjoyed. God gifted me with fifty-four years of precious kisses, and now he has brought me this new friend and maybe a new love. I think I am brave enough to handle it.

I lean in, smelling his aftershave, feeling his gray hair with my arthritic fingers. I know it will be alright. My hazy, gray eyes close, my thin, pink lips part, and I let the young woman inside get lost in another *first kiss*.

# Eaten Up

You know that saying: "If Mom ain't happy, ain't nobody happy"? Well, in our house, if Dad ain't happy, life sucks. Three things I can say about my dad. One, he's fat. His flappy, chapped jowls jiggle when he chews like a chipmunk stuffing his cheeks for winter.

Second, he's angry. I don't mean just right now but all the time. It's like he's always at the point of a rumbling volcano, and Mom, Aaron and I don't know when he'll just blow. I used to think he was just pissed off at the world, but as I get older I realize…it's me. I'm the problem—*no gold stars for me, Dad*. I don't dare look at him across the dinner table. I don't need to see his eyes to feel his disapproval or to know how it affects the whole family.

"Finish up, Aaron."

His words spurt out along with some mashed potatoes before he wipes his whiskered chin and glares toward my plate.

"You, too, young lady. We don't waste food in this house."

*Carrie, Dad. The name's Carrie.*

And that brings me to the third thing: Dad is not really my dad. Aaron is not really my brother. Mom is not really my mom. I'm adopted.

Adopted, as in, picked up and brought in from somewhere else, like a pinch hitter, a substitute, a stand-in for the real thing.

Kids at school identify themselves in some way—geek, diva, jock, Goth. And we identify them in some way, too—tool, ho, ratchet, stoner.

Me, I think I'm pretty enough—in a *fat girl* sort of way. It's okay; I don't mind being fat. I can still kick my brother's butt at hoops.

And I can drive a car, only nobody's supposed to know that except my best friend Andrea, whose older sister took us out in the cow pasture last summer when I was only thirteen. Luckily, for all of us, there were no trees to hit or ditches to fall in.

I'm also a decent student, even in high school; I get A's and some B's.

But mostly…I'm just adopted. I was a local baby, adopted by the Fleischman family when I was only six months old, and that's all I know. It was a *closed* adoption—at least to me. My parents know all about it.

I don't really belong. I'm not really *at home* here. I'm not really a part of this family. I'm the adopted kid, like a fake. Only sometimes, it feels like I'm the real one and my family is the fake. So fake.

I have no roots, no identity. As far as I'm concerned, being adopted is the biggest thing about me, and at fourteen years old, they still won't tell me the whole story. I've only asked them, like, fifty times.

"When you're eighteen," my mom said one morning over breakfast, as she did whenever I brought the subject up. "Then we will tell you who your birth parents are. Now finish your eggs—you're going to miss the bus."

I don't feel like eating tonight. I feel full, like I've snatched up this secret thing that hangs in the air and swallowed it whole. It scrapes and cuts its way down my throat and blows up in my stomach—this stupid, stinking secret that everyone's in on except for me.

There's other crap we don't talk about, too, like anger, denial, and grief; bitterness, boredom, and disappointment; unmet expectations from life and each other; Dad's irritation with life in general and with me in particular.

Through hooded eyebrows—my Batman face, Aaron calls it—I look over at Mom across from me, concentrating on pushing her peas onto the fork with her dinner roll. *Gold stars, Mom! You're very focused.*

"So, Mom," I start in, "we're doing this project on our family tree for school, and I was just wondering…"

She ignores me.

"It's okay, Mom," I say in my most nonchalant voice, "I can take it. You can trust me with the truth."

She takes a drink of water and looks at Dad.

"Look, I'm gonna find out sooner or later, and you would rather I learn it from you, instead of on the street somewhere."

Aaron snorts beside me.

"That's enough, young lady," Dad says.

"Have another roll, dear," Mom says. I don't know if she means me or Dad. Neither one of us takes her up on the offer.

The sky has turned the color of macaroni and cheese. The sun's rays shine in through the dining room window and across the table, but it does nothing to brighten the mood.

My mouth feels heavy. It's an effort just to close my mouth and chew. I shovel my carrots in and grind my teeth together like a cow. Some of it falls to my plate, like a puppet eating a cookie. I feel like laughing. I can just hear Mom's reaction: "Carrie! That's so inappropriate!" That would irritate the heck out of her if she was looking.

But she's not looking. I don't laugh.

Shielding my face with my glass of milk, I steal a sideways glance at Aaron next to me. He is inhaling his food. He eats like that every time we sit down at the dinner table. It's like nobody's fed him since last summer or something. He's gotten bigger. He was always big—fat like the rest of us—but now he's big-big, not just fat-big. It looks okay on him actually. I think he's on the football team this year. If he's not, he should be. Then he could get a big, fat scholarship and get out of this stinking hole.

I can tell he's not really here though. He's eating his food but not really tasting anything. He's sitting in the chair next to me. But he's really someplace else. Lucky jerk—figuring a way out of the *all-important family dinner forced-togetherness* time. *Five stars, brother.*

I study his sandy brown eyebrows and matching mop of hair. I try to figure out where he is in his mind—maybe I can go there, too. Playing his drums in the garage, where it won't bother Mom and Dad. Riding his beat-up bike over in the church parking lot. Throwing rocks at the rusted mailboxes out on County Road 42 from the back of Jeffrey's dad's pick-up. Over at the Burger Barn checking out girls who are pretending not to check him out, in return. If only one of them would take him away from all this. And take me, too.

It's so dang quiet in here except for all the placid chewing around me. It's annoying—the silence, the routine, the suffocating, eggshell-stepping my mother does all the time, even when she's eating.

Stabbing the meat with my fork, I start spinning it around in front of my face like a twizzle stick. Then I sit up and clear my throat.

"Did you know pig thyroid hormone is a lot like human thyroid hormone, so they use it for thyroid replacement in humans? We learned about that in Metcalf's class today."

They all pretend not to hear me.

"So when we eat pig, it's like we're eating something close to our own kind. It's a bit cannibalistic, don't you think?" Then I take a big bite of my pork and kind of maw it with my teeth. It's so great because I know it's really annoying my dad.

I think I surprised my brother though. He looks over and says, "Nice one, Care Bear," which is about as good a high-five as I'm going to get from him.

Mom looks pretty freaked out. She's getting so intense over those carrots now, like a rabid dog or something.

Dad is not impressed. He's a tougher nut to crack. Instead of blowing his top and getting it over with like other dads, he keeps his ire stuffed up in his cheeks along with the partially chewed pork roast and carrots. Then he lets it out a little at a time, like spitting all over you.

One look at him now, and I know it's coming. Even though I'm expecting it, it will catch me off guard, like when you bite your tongue and then a little while later, you do it again.

Picking at my carrots with my fork irritates him. So I keep doing it.

"It's amazing what you can find on the internet these days. Names, dates, all on public record."

Not even a raised eyebrow. *Four stars, Dad.*

"I flunked my chemistry exam last week. Geometry, too. My Spanish teacher says she thinks I can apply myself more, if I would just find the right motivation."

The vein in his neck isn't bulging yet, but his face looks a little red around the edges.

"My boyfriend *really* motivates me," I say.

"Boyfriend?" Mom says. "This is the first I've heard about it."

Oh, she *is* listening.

"Yeah, well, he's not really my boyfriend, just a friend I guess, but we've been talking, you know, getting pretty *close.*"

Her eyes look like they are going to bug out of her head. She stares at me, waiting. Dad is looking at his plate, but he's stopped chewing. He's waiting, too.

"He's a dropout; he comes by the practice field and hangs out during lunch. Looks like he's been around, you know. Pretty cute actually."

Aaron chokes on his milk, trying to hold back a laugh. He knows me too well.

"You're full of crap, Care."

"Am I?" I say in my innocent voice.

"He doesn't sound like an appropriate choice, Carrie," Mom says. She's afraid. She's a little afraid I'll quit school and run off and become a…what?

But she's a lot afraid I'll run off and do IT and get pregnant and…

Dad's trying hard to ignore me. I think it makes him feel powerful somehow to puke all over me with antagonism. It helps him forget that he's not a big shot—he's just like the rest of us, shuffled along by life, herded through the fencing from one stop to the next, like cows to the slaughter.

Hunched over his near empty plate, his posture says, it doesn't matter to him. His expression says, *I* don't matter to him.

"What about you, Dad? What do you have to say?"

Nothing.

"Don't you care about my grades? Don't you care about my boyfriend? Don't you care about anything?" I push my chair back from the table, scraping it as loudly as possible across the wood floor. I hope it leaves a mark.

"What am I, after all? Just your *adopted* daughter, just the freakish other person who eats at your table and sleeps in your house and shares your last name."

"Your mother's a drug addict, Carrie!" It's Mom's voice, cutting, icy, like red, bony, frozen meat.

I can't move. I can't swallow. I can't breathe. I can't pull my eyes away from Dad's face to look at Mom. I stand still, like a cat, staring, waiting. I need to hear the rest of the story.

"Some guy she met in a bar, I guess, just one of many with her up in Chicago, doing drugs, practically living on the streets. She got pregnant." Mom shrugs her shoulders. "He meant nothing to her, and…"

*You meant nothing to her. I dare you to say it, Mom. You meant nothing to her. Say it. Say it.*

"…we took you in."

Dad blinks and I can finally let out a breath.

*We took you in.* I wonder whose idea that was. Maybe I was forced upon them, the decision guilted upon them by some random aunt butting-in, like those documentaries about being vegetarian that are supposed to make you feel wretched and shameful for eating meat.

I am barely able to get the words past the lump in my

throat. "So who is she? How do you…?"

"She's my sister, Carrie. And she's still nothing but a messed-up drug addict. Drink your milk."

My eyes flicker to the glass on the table. Mom failed to notice that it's empty. Empty.

Dad clears his throat and says, "The barn needs to be swept out, young lady. It won't keep till morning."

I walk toward the sink in a daze. I drop my mostly-full plate into the sink and watch the peas roll out into the little net-thingy that is supposed to keep food from going down the drain and clogging up the garbage disposal.

I start to walk away, but instead, I turn back toward the sink, lift up the net-thingy and use my fork to push all the remains of my dinner down into the disposal. I'm not worried about the food, I've got more in my room. I'm not worried about the disposal either. Mom will keep plugging away, whether it breaks or not. She's used to working with broke things.

Downstairs, my bedroom seems strange to me. The work shoes I slip on and the old sweatshirt I've worn for two years seem like someone else's clothes. I find a couple of chocolate bars and some snack cakes in my dresser and stuff them into the front pocket of my sweatshirt. I'm careful to slip out through the backdoor. I don't want to see Mom at the sink, fussing over the dishes, trying not to cry, trying not to think.

I don't care where Dad is.

I head toward the barn. Dust is hanging in the air out behind the house. I know it is Aaron, headed out somewhere on his bike. He'll be home before dark.

The sky is starting to redden; darkness will swallow the meadow up in half an hour's time. I step into the barn. The animal and crap smell is heavy and suffocating, but in a good way. The animals recognize my smell, too, and make muffled grunts of contentment.

I am wanted here. I sit on a bale of hay in the darkness, eat both snack cakes quickly, and hide the wrappers back in my pocket. Taking a deep breath and waiting for the rush of sugar to hit my bloodstream, I feel for the two chocolate bars still in my pocket. *My secret stash of sweets for whenever I want—gold stars, Carrie, gold stars.*

I feel full and good out here. I think I can shovel crap for a little while longer.

# Attitude Adjustment

**Monday, September 10**—Grandma got me this journal since I was starting third grade. It wasn't even my birthday or nothing. Mom says the best way I can say thank you is to write in it. I hope it's not a diary because only girls do that. At least only one kid elbowed me today in the lunch line. "No cuts!" he shouted and Missus Kinney sent me to stand in the back of the line with the pigtail girl that picks her nose and smells bad.

**Thursday, September 13**—Missus Kinney yells the whole day long. Mom says I should pray for her that she'll feel better. I'll pray she gets an attitude adjustment. Science is cool though! We got to explode some stuff today and it was all oozy and everything. I bumped the table and some of it got on my shoe, but I just wiped it off on the carpet. Missus Kinney didn't see.

**Friday, September 21**—Woohoo! Weekend! No more school! And woohoo! I found a quarter on the playground today.

**Monday, September 24**—Sometimes the only good thing about my day is the joke Mom puts in my lunch. I stood up for Danny in our class today. He's the slow kid who sits in the front row. The kid with the sharp elbows called Danny a "retard" and was making fun so I shoved that boy on the playground and nobody caught me. Serves him right.

**Thursday, September 27**—Danny sat by me at lunch and I helped him open his milk. He doesn't talk very much but he smiles plenty. The boys' bathroom smells bad. And God, help Missus Kinney like Mom was saying, cause she's so mad with me and everybody in the whole class. ALL THE TIME!!!!!!!!!

**Tuesday, October 2**—The girl that picks her nose and smells bad sat by me at lunch today. I didn't want her sitting there since she's a girl but I didn't want her to feel bad, so I just pretended she didn't smell and kept my nose full of peanut butter sandwich.

**Monday, October 8**—That girl that picks her nose and smells bad doesn't have a mom. She told me cause her mom ran away from home and never loved her anymore. That girl told me her daddy cries sometimes. I told her the joke from my lunch after that. She cracked up! This weekend Grandpa's taking me fishing and I get to put my own worm on the hook.

**Monday, October 15**—It rained and rained. Grandpa said that made the fishing better and it was awesome cause we caught sixteen whole fish! Two of them were mine, too, and I got to help gut them before we cooked them in the camper. Fire cooking's more fun, but since it rained us out, we cooked in the camper.

**Tuesday, October 16**—God, Missus Kinney needs cheered up an awful lot. Today she looked all red and cry-ey, like Mom looks sometimes, when she watches her movies. I climbed to the top of the rope in gym today and touched the ceiling—woohoo! I got bologna in my lunch—not woohoo!

**Friday, October 19**—Danny laughs real loud and he likes the jokes Mom puts in my lunch. I'm glad he's feeling better now because he's slow and the big boys still act ugly to him. Only when I'm there, they just keep their traps shut!! That girl that smells bad went to the school nurse today and when she came back at lunch time, she smelled better. She gave me a candy the nurse had given her. It was cherry. For Halloween this year, I'm going to be a race car driver. Missus Kinney will probably dress up as a witch, only she doesn't have to dress up.

**Wednesday, October 24**—Mom read this and said that wasn't very nice. I said it was true (and private besides). She told me again about the praying. So God, you know, help Missus Kinney out (because she really is like a witch sometimes.) She yelled at me for sharpening my pencil today! It wasn't my fault it kept breaking so many times.

**Monday, October 29**—Halloween is almost here!!!! I am going to fill up two whole pumpkins with candy this year, maybe even three!! I just know it.

**Thursday, November 1**—That girl who sits next to me, her name's Caroline. She didn't get to go trick-or-treating, only I don't know why. Danny had two candies in his lunch, Whoppers and Smarties, so I know *he* got to go trick-or-treating.

**Friday, November 2**—I brought some of my extra candy in a paper bag stuffed in my pocket and sneaked it to Caroline. It was just the ones I don't like really, like the Tootsie Rolls and the peanut M&M's, cause she's still a girl anyways. I threw in one Blow-Pop though, just to be nice.

**Monday, November 5**—Missus Kinney needs you bad, God, but I think she might be getting a tiny bit nicer. Be with Danny, too, cause I might not always be around to look out for him. And that girl Caroline. And her dad. And her mom, wherever she is. Amen. Today we watched a movie about not smoking. The lungs were super gross!

**Tuesday, November 6**—Math is super cool because we had this substitute today and he did all this fun stuff and I really liked all the stuff he did cause it was really fun. Only Science is still my favorite.

**Wednesday, November 7**—We still have the sub, which is great because you know how Missus Kinney is kind of not great and everything. And yes, I'm still praying, Mom, so if you're reading this, don't be mad because I'm doing what you said. God, help me to like Missus Kinney more, Amen.

**Thursday, November 8**—Missus Kinney is back today and sent home notes to all our parents about conferences! Only one week to act really, really good. I forgot my lunch at home so I had tacos and applesauce at school, which was pretty good actually.

**Thursday, November 15**—Russell is a new kid today and I invited him to sit with Caroline and Danny and me since he's the new kid. He shared his Cheetos with the rest of us, and I told him my joke. "What's more dangerous than pulling a shark's tooth? Giving a porcupine a back rub!" We all high-fived each other.

*************

Mrs. Kinney and Zachary's mother greet each other at the door and walk to the short round table in the center of the room.

"Mrs. Wheeler? I'm so glad to see you. Please have a seat. I have to tell you: Zachary is a real prize in this class. He excels at math, he loves science, and he is a very respectful little boy. Here's some of his work that he chose to keep in his Star Folder.

"Mrs. Wheeler, this is the thing—Zachary truly astounds me! Honestly, the best words I can think of to describe him are *guardian angel*. There are several very needy children in this classroom and somehow, Zach has zeroed in on them and has put them under his protective care. One little boy is differently abled, and Zach stood up to some of the tougher boys in the class and shielded this particular boy from their ugly comments and behavior.

"That's not all. There's a little girl. I know. Boys this age usually won't have anything to do with girls, but Zachary befriended this particular girl and she comes from such a difficult home situation.

"I don't know what to say, Mrs. Wheeler. I've seen the three of them together. Oh, even the new boy who just arrived in my classroom—he has found a friend in Zachary. They play together, eat lunch together. Ma'am, just between you and me, I've seen Zachary praying with them before they eat their lunch.

"It's more than cute, ma'am. It has been life-changing for these children. I...I don't know what to say. Even for me...

"I've been having a really rough year myself...my husband...my divorce was finalized last week. I've been having a really hard time. Things have been falling apart little by little for the last year...

"But over the last couple of weeks, I have felt more, I don't know what to call it—peaceful, maybe. I think it has a lot to do with your son.

"I know I'm not anyone's favorite teacher, but I feel...and watching your son...well, I've definitely undergone some kind of attitude adjustment. I just know somehow that everything is going to be okay. I hope I can become the kind of teacher Zachary and the other children deserve.

"I'm sorry. I don't mean to blubber like this. The bottom line is this: he's a really special little boy, and I thank you for sharing him with me."

\*\*\*\*\*\*\*\*\*\*\*\*

**Friday, November 16**—Mom just came home from conferences with this weird look on her face. She didn't say anything, only she looked all cry-ey like she gets sometimes, and she gave me a big hug. Moms are so weird.

# The Crossing Guard

*Danged wind,* Sam grumbled inwardly as crinkly, brown leaves swooped in front of his crinkly, brown face before settling in the intersection where he stood. The wind nipped at his ears and nose. Frost clung to the thick salt-and-pepper mustache that curled around his upper lip, and his whiskered-cheeks burned.

*Danged arthritis,* he thought as he squeezed his fingers tighter around the stop sign. Irritated and squinting in the harsh winter light, Sam hardly noticed the small children walking by on their way to school.

Under his wooly eyebrows, Sam's good and bad days were mapped out all over his leathery face. Lines engraved by time and circumstance left him looking as if he had been pistol-whipped at high noon by a vicious scoundrel from long ago. Though he had been wizened and grizzened by crueler circumstances than these, he had fallen prey to a sour disposition this morning, just because of the nasty weather. The realization irritated him even more.

Sam's beefy hands fit snug in their worn, leather gloves. With his right hand, he pulled at the wooly collar, bringing it nearer to his ears. In his left hand, Sam held up a stop sign, its white letters gleamed in the intense, winter light.

Sometimes Sam felt appreciated by passersby, both young and old. They exchanged smiles and *good mornings* as they moved past him toward the neighborhood school. On those days, the weight of the sign, held aloft in the crosswalk, did not trouble his aching shoulders and arthritic elbows and wrists.

Days like today, however, he just felt like an old fool. Some children and harried parents rushed past in a blur. Others meandered by in a slow growl, their faces tight with unspoken thoughts and feelings. The stop sign weighed him down. The message was aimed at him: *Stop. Quit. Go home. Stick a fork in ya—yer done.*

"G'morning, Mr. Sam," a little boy beamed as he approached the crossing guard. His shoes were untied and his clothes looked like they'd been slept in, or at least worn several days in a row. His black face and wooly head were bare in the bitter cold as he walked alone. Sam had noted the change over the last few months.

"G'morning, Mr. Sam," the boy repeated. Mr. Sam's mustache twitched as it crept up into an almost smile at one corner of his mouth. The first-grader could hear the scritchy-scratchy sound of the whiskers on the old man's face as it rubbed against the raised collar of his coat. The boy bobbed happily under Mr. Sam's protective beacon.

*Mr. Sam is like my Granddad.* The thought came to the boy, not with words, but like a filmstrip playing behind his eyes. The youngster thought of his own granddad mussing his short black hair, just as Mr. Sam had sometimes done. In his mind's eye, his granddad was laughing with those same wrinkled, crinkled eyes, tickling him and embracing him and telling him fantastic tales as he tucked him into bed at night.

Whenever this bear of a man would pat his shoulder and say, "Good morning, son," with that low, wonderfully growly voice of his, it was just like Granddad would do it, and the thought comforted the boy like warm oatmeal with lots of butter and brown sugar.

For the moment it did not matter that there was no real oatmeal this morning, or even crackers and juice for breakfast.

It did not matter that Granddad no longer cuddled him or told him stories since he was always in bed with those awful needles and tubes.

It did not matter about that yucky lady who looked after Granddad, the one who was always shooing him out of the room.

It did not matter that his Mama left so early for work

every morning and came home so worn out at night, she could barely take care of herself, much less fix him supper, a hot bath, and a tuck-in.

It did not matter that no one at school really knew anything about his life at home.

*It doesn't matter, not really. It'll all come right soon.*

The six-year-old doggedly carried his heavy burden over both shoulders as if the weight of his little world could be stuffed into his backpack along with an unmatched glove, an old spelling test, and a leftover sandwich he was saving for later, for when he got really, really hungry.

*It's alright 'cause Granddad's gonna get well and Mama's gonna quit work and stay home and take care of me again like it used to be.*

Sam stopped the boy on the curb and set down his sign. Without a word, he bent down and tied the boy's wayward shoelaces. Then with a firm pat on the shoulder and a nod of his gray head, he shooed the youngster on toward school. His bare hand waving in the wind, the boy hollered back over his shoulder, "See ya later, Mr. Sam."

\*\*\*\*\*\*\*\*\*\*\*\*\*

Sam had forgotten his sunglasses again this morning.

He wished he had them now. Tears came to his eyes unbidden. His face felt hot despite the cold. He grumbled to himself.

Squeezing his eyes, Sam tried to push the tears back in with a gloved thumb and index finger. He wondered about the boy and why he, who had once been so neat in pressed pants, warm coat and tied shoes, now seemed so unkempt. *Where was the young mother who walked with him every morning?* He sent up a short, silent prayer on the boy's behalf before returning to his post.

Several older girls walked by. These were middleschoolers, dressed in their matching skinny jeans and tee shirts. Sam held the sign up for them, too. *No coats,* Sam noted. Nothing had changed since he was a youngster, often hurrying to school with no socks and uncombed hair or leaving the lunch box and math book on the kitchen table next to his empty cereal bowl.

*Mr. Nasty* approached the intersection in his car, as he did every morning, and glared at Sam. Sam could feel his impatience as mothers hurried along with their strollers, fussing at their preschool children to speed up. *Mr. Nasty* probably didn't bother leaving for work on time in the first place, and then created stress for everyone along his commute. Sam stood his ground in the road until a few more students hurried through. The man showed no patience for Sam with his orange vest and red stop sign. In return, Sam showed no sympathy for the man's irritation.

Sam saved his unspoken sympathies for moms and kids that came his way. One young mom approached, a coat hastily thrown over flannel pajamas. Her hair was awry and her face crumpled by stress. She always looked like a train wreck and Sam worried over her.

An older woman was walking her grandchildren to school. Sam bristled inwardly when she passed by. With too much make-up and her lavender polyester pants so tight they were practically cutting her in half, she looked too showy for her age, like she was trying too hard. And for what? For him? He wondered. When she looked up at him, he grimaced.

"Sam? Sam! What's wrong with you? I said, 'Good morning.' Can't you offer a proper greeting to an old woman?"

"Morning," he sputtered, looking away to the children. The little girl had two tight braids, and Sam could practically smell the soap on the little boy's well-scrubbed face. Someone at home was making sure these kids were well-fed and well-groomed. Sam had to give the grandmother credit for that much.

"Have a good day, Sam," she sing-songed as she

passed, her voice and eyes softening. How could he know she fixed up her hair just before leaving the house? How could he know she put on lipstick and a girdle—*what'd they call them nowadays—spanx?*—just for this moment, just for this few seconds each morning before school? She reflected on the rendezvous in the crosswalk all day, as she sat alone at her kitchen table with a tall glass of Coca-Cola and her Las Vegas ash tray filled with half-smoked Virginia Slims.

*How kind Sam is to notice me, even if he doesn't like to show it. And how thoughtful he is to my grandchildren! I feel so protected in his care. He practically embraces me every step I take across the street. Someday I will walk back that way and look up into his eyes. He will look into mine with that rough, manly way of his and accept an invitation to come have some coffee. I will have cookies ready for him, too. No, a pie would be better. That's it. I'll make a pie.*

\*\*\*\*\*\*\*\*\*\*\*\*

Sam saw everything during the forty-five minute tour at his intersection—some kids looked happy as larks, while others looked neglected or older than their years. Without words, so many of them seemed to say, *I have already seen and endured too much in this life.*

One boy walked by, right before the school bell rang. Every day he dressed in black—dark shirt, dark pants, and non-descript jacket. Sam guessed he was trying to camouflage the rolls that hung around his arms, his chest, and his middle. He must be trying to hide his weight or just plain hide. His face drooped with weight and so did his heart, it seemed. He was not an elementary student. He walked on up the hill to the middle school, a few blocks east of Sam's spot.

As always, Sam held up the sign for him whether the boy thought he needed it or not. Sam also said his usual *good morning* whether the boy wanted it or not.

Sam could not know that the boy waited for that *good morning* as he passed. It was the first greeting of the morning and one of the only kindnesses the boy would receive over the course of his whole day.

Sam could not know the boy's heart had rotted to its core with bitterness and grief. He was numb with hate, and Sam's morning nod and occasional pat on the shoulder meant life instead of death to this lost middle-schooler who passed by every day on his way to hell.

Sam could not know that the boy's hands were in his pockets, not to keep them out of the cold but to keep them out of sight. There in the darkness of his pocket, he fiddled with the knife he kept there; and in the darkness of his heart he fiddled with the idea of ending it all for himself or someone else.

"Morning." Sam looked down at the boy and smiled, really smiled, for the first time that morning.

"M-m-morning," the boy choked out as he passed under the sign. He seemed surprised by his own voice. Sam was surprised, too. The boy had never spoken to him before.

From the sidewalk he looked back at Sam for a moment. Sam nodded and the boy turned around, took a deep breath, and kept heading up the hill. *Not today,* the boy thought to himself. *Not today.*

\*\*\*\*\*\*\*\*\*\*\*\*\*

The school bell rang. Sam studied his watch. He looked up and down the streets. Kids were in their classrooms. Parents were at home or at work. Sam was glad his tour of duty was over. He began his walk home, looking forward to being out of the cold, putting up his feet, and taking a nap in his chair.

Sam's frost-crusted mustache cracked a little with a smile. Whether appreciated or not, Sam was *not* done. He was needed—somewhere at least. He would press on regardless of the scowling faces, the blistering cold winds, or the heaviness of the sign he would hold aloft again tomorrow morning.

# Remembering Romance

"Here's your juice, honey. Take your pills."

Ramona looked at the plate. She didn't see the pills, only the little blue flowers that circled the plate.

"Those little guys were everywhere, weren't they?" Her voice was dreamy, her expression distant.

Howard's *uh-huh* came dutifully from the kitchen. He was already busy with his breakfast dishes. One plate, one cup, one fork. Maybe later he could get her to eat some oatmeal or a boiled egg.

"Blue bells…? Don't you remember, Howard? They were everywhere. We'd be driving along the highway in our old truck, and there they'd be —little blue flowers as far as the eye could see." Her voice trailed off again.

At one time Howard's heart would have warmed at the memory of that old truck he'd bought for a song from his Daddy's best friend, Mr. Stanley.

"Weeeell," Mr. Stanley had drawled, leaning back on his heels with his thumbs tucked in his bib overalls, "I'll tell you what: I owe your daddy some money and between that and the repairs that I know you'll have to do on this old truck, I'll give her to you for, ohhh…whad-daya say, seventy-five dollars? Will that work for ya, young man?"

Nineteen-year-old Howard's '*yes sir*' was so enthusiastic, his neck felt it would snap like that of a chicken caught for supper. With a truck, a job, and most of his education finished up at the university, he could finally go a'courting Ramona O'Shea.

But on this day, Howard wasn't reflecting on the past. He wasn't listening to Ramona talk to herself. He was hand-drying his last dish, putting it in the cupboard, and mentally going over the doctors he had to call, the meds he had to administer, the groceries he had to get, and the clothes he had to wash.

Howard closed his eyes and grimaced. Ramona had a pair of blue pants, a couple of polyester blouses that still fit, and a favorite sweater. When these began to smell of sweat, food, and age, he knew he had to wash them, and there would be a fight when he tried to get Ramona to wear something else.

"Where are my clothes?" she would accuse. "What have you done with my clothes?" He wanted to hide in the garage and pull at his gray hair every time the subject came up. The first few times, he did just that.

Forty-five minutes to wash and thirty minutes to dry.

If he got desperate, he could distract her with television and sweets. Funny, how she would remember about the clothes, and her indictment of him would flare up once more.

Four and a half years ago, Howard had stopped smiling and stopped daydreaming. The day he was told his wife was losing her memory, he started losing his mind. He went through the motions of going to work each morning, doing his duty and going home, but there were no *good mornings* to anyone, no nods of affirmation. Howard's heart had dried up like an apple long forgotten in the back window of the Buick.

*I'm a crusty old man now,* he thought, *but what am I supposed to do?* Howard hated not knowing what to expect, not knowing when it would get worse, when she would forget him altogether, when *she* would dry up.

He tried not to be hard, heavy-hearted or heavy-handed. He could be rude, frustrated, and plain old hateful. He hated himself for it.

Ramona was still sitting at the table, most of her pills still on the plate. Her curls were limp and greasy. Showering—another battle to be faced.

He headed toward the bathroom and turned on the light. When had he grown so gray? Even his skin looked gray.

"Do I look as bad as I feel?" his wife had asked him one day years ago when their girls were young.

"Worse," he had said with a wink. Those years were rough, always juggling, scurrying, and shouting the kids through their morning. All day long Ramona would beat herself up about having been too hard on them, about having been too unsympathetic to their childish ways. But when the evening came, there she would be again, scolding and fussing to get them through chores and homework.

Howard sighed. He wished now he had stepped in more to help her, to ease her burden in some way. The circumstances would not have been any less frustrating —that hour of purgatory just before dinner when everything had to be done and everyone had to be attended to —but Ramona's heart would have been lighter just to have another player on the team. The few times he had offered to do the dishes or finish up an atom model with one of the kids, his wife's relief was palpable, a living and breathing thing that pleasantly hovered between them. What he wouldn't give to see that gleam again, to feel her eyes on him—seeing him, knowing him, and being grateful for him.

*I didn't notice her hectic need. I didn't bother to notice.* He was too busy with his own agenda, making sure that whatever he wanted to get done got done and not considering what *her* priorities might be. Whenever his conscience sat him down for one of their little talks, he defended his behavior and choices. He told himself it was for the best, that he was looking out for his family's best interests, that he was being the provider. Meanwhile, Ramona, maneuvering like a juggler, held everything together—their girls, their home, and even their marriage. Now he was the one juggling and holding things together and doing the dishes.

Howard sighed again, turned off the light, and left the bathroom. He did not want to look anymore. He hated himself then, and he hated himself now.

He grabbed a jacket from the closet. *A quick walk to the mail boxes at the end of the road—that would help. A little break before I have to get to the to-do list,* he thought.

"Ramona? I'll be just outside. Ramona?"

"Okay, Howard." She had moved away from the flowers on the plate. Now she was studying the bills on the table, reading each word out loud. "St. Anthony's Hospital Billing Department. Oh that's interesting. I don't remember anybody named Anthony? Do you know him? He works at the hospital."

Howard let the screen door slam behind him. He remembered the screen door slamming on his wife many a time before. The brawling and bawling between his wife and their two teenage daughters years ago had usually been about clothes.

"Mama, you just don't care," stormed one.

"I'll be fine, Mama, but my hair is gonna look so gross if I have to wear that stupid ski cap," complained the other. Howard stayed neutral—on the outside. *It was just clothes. What's the big deal?*

When his daughters weren't looking, he would wink at his wife. That calmed her. When his wife was not looking, he would wink at his daughters. That made them madder. Ramona eventually found other battles worth fighting about like curfew or car dates with boys. He let her handle those, too.

Howard was in no hurry today. He wanted to get away for a while. He wanted to forget.

He walked past one neighbor's rose bushes, barely green yet.

He walked by a woman walking her dog. She waved. He smiled.

He walked past his friend's white pick-up with the rusted out flat bed.

He remembered another truck now. They were on a date. Ramona was perched on his lap in the backseat of an old Ford. Another fellow sat there beside him in the same pleasant predicament with his girl; Howard could no longer remember his name.

Ramona's arms were around Howard's neck. Her brown curls rested on his shoulder. She spoke something right in his ear, but with the windows down and the wind blowing into his face, he didn't catch it.

"WHAT'S THAT?" Howard hollered, scrunching up his face in an effort to hear her.

She lifted her head up, "WHY DON'T WE GET MARRIED?"

He stared at her, disbelieving, thrilled. "THAT SOUNDS LIKE A GOOD IDEA!"

They got married, got a house, and got a dog. They made love, made kids, and made-up after fighting. They grew a garden, grew up, grew old, and…what?

Howard took a deep breath. His conscience was ready to sit down for one of their little talks again. He headed back to the house without checking the mail.

Opening the screen door and finding his wife still at the table, he knelt down on the carpet in front of her. Not bothering to remove his coat, he took her hands in his own. They were warm.

"Ramona?"

"Hi, Howard."

"Ramona, do you remember when you asked me to

marry you?"

"Did I? That was a good idea, wasn't it?"

"Yes, Ramona, it was." Howard studied his wife's face. The lines he and the girls had put there were lovely and framed by curls.

"Ramona?"

"Howard."

"Do you remember the bluebells?"

"What bluebells?"

"The bluebells that grew all around when we would go driving in my old truck."

"As far as the eye could see."

"Yes, that's right, Ramona. And you know what else?"

"What's that, Howard?"

"You were a great mother who raised two beautiful girls."

"Those were good times," she said.

"Yes, they were."

"I'm so glad I married you, Howard."

"Me, too, Ramona."

Howard stood up and kissed his wife's forehead. "Take your pills, honey, and finish your juice."

"Okay, Howard."

Howard looked at the to-do list posted on the fridge.

The first thing was laundry. *What's the big deal,* he thought to himself. *It's just clothes.*

Howard's throat got thick. A weak smile crossed his lips. She may no longer remember, but he would never forget.

His conscience winked at him and gave him a gentle shove toward the laundry room.

# Running Amuck

*Running amuck.* Ms. Vieira's words to the class penetrated my heart like a knife. I snapped. Sliding out from my desk, I moved toward the door before my mother's voice inside my head could stop me. Before she could call my name, scold me in her Old-world Spanish, and command me to sit down and be a good girl.

"Magdalena!" I whirled around to see Ms. Vieira's shocked face. Her blue eyes were wide at first, and then I saw something else there. *Understanding? Or pity! Oh Lord God, not that. Please don't let any of these frigging gringos feel sorry for me.*

I looked at all of them then. Kids who had been taking notes or texting or sleeping. Guys I feared, girls I hated. Blacks, whites, browns, rich, poor, all looking back at me. Looking, but not seeing. Not really seeing me.

And then I ran.

Out of the room, out of the school, down the road, and I'm still running. Running and I can't stop. Running and I won't stop. Not this time. I'm running amuck.

I don't know what it means, but somehow it fits what

they all think of me—dirty, clumsy, lazy, just one of those frigging Mexicans, always screwing things up for the rest of us. *Go back home, you filthy beaners! Get the hell away from us!*

Who do they think they are? Stupid jerks judging me with their nasty, hateful words. Why am I the one who is made to feel this way? *Amuck,* like something sticky or dirty. Like I've got mud on my hands, blood on my hands. I should go away—just run away and keep on running.

Running from those boxes and the girls who put me in them. *Girls like them* that glare and dare and put *girls like us* in little boxes with labels marked 'other.' *Girls like us* lumped together because we're freaks. Girls with glasses or braces, freckles or acne, red hair or side-parts or big breasts. Girls who got their periods late or early. Fat girls, dirty girls, poor girls, brown girls. There we all are—the freaks, left to die in our little boxes marked 'other.'

Running from the gringos who chase me at school—stupid, idiot boys who think just because I've got big brown boobs means it's a free for all—free for touching, free for grabbing, free for taking. Like I'm everybody's own personal amusement park ride. Can't keep their stinking hands to themselves, the frigging bastards. F-you, f-you all, I'm not free for the taking. I will not be taken.

I'm running scared. I don't care if there's nothing to run to. I don't care if it sucks out there like it does here. I've just gotta go—get far from here—even if I'm scared.

When I was eight years old and my family first moved to this stinking hole—it was scary then. At that time there weren't any other Mexicans or blacks or anyone brown in this small town in the Midwest. Only white boys as far as the eye could see. I think Mama was scared, too. She hardly left the house except to go to church.

Poor whites lived in the trailer court where we lived, and this boy and his cousin were chasing me one day. With squirt guns. They said it was a game; it wasn't. They chased me until I fell and cried. They squirted me till they ran out of water, till I couldn't see anymore. When I got up, my leg was bleeding, my dress was torn.

The blood was running down my leg, but that wasn't the scariest part. The laughing and the chasing and the talk I didn't understand back then. I didn't ask to be included in their game. Boys are always playing games. That day and many days like it have left me with scars, like the one still on my knee.

I run past houses and cars. Drivers on the road slow down to stare. They seem to know I'm not supposed to be out here—out of school, out of Mexico. I try not to see them. I keep running.

When I was a little kid, there was always Mama. Hers was the face I saw in the morning when I woke up for school. Hers was the face I watched as she laughed and told stories over the stove where she fixed coffee and tortillas and fried potatoes for breakfast. Hers was the face I held with my eyes in church, watching her pray, seeing her faith.

My brothers were there, too, with their sneering faces and their grubby, filthy, dirty hands. They were fat and mean. That's what made them so frightening to everyone, frightening to me.

There was a slow boy at the bus stop in those days— retarded, they called him. He was in my grade—a nice boy who played with me even though I was brown. One day the news came back to Mama that my brothers were bullying him. She cried when they got home. I think she was ashamed because of what everyone said.

And then she beat them. She told them if it was true, they had better stop, go to the priest, and pray for forgiveness. She said, they'd better be good or she'd tell Papa when he got home. She never told Papa; Mama wouldn't do that. Not about the boy and not about the other things either.

I run past my old bus stop where I used to take the bus to school with the other kids. There was a dead cat there one day, laying bloody in the grass. Everyone said it was my brothers who did it. Mama beat them and scolded them for that, too, just to be sure. What everyone said about my brothers, about the boy and the cat and the other stuff—I know my brothers, and everyone was probably right.

My side aches, but I clutch at it and keep running. I turn a corner and run by a yard sale. The old woman who sits in a lawn chair is smoking and looking. She sees me and waves with a gap-tooth smile. I'm breathing so hard, I don't think to wave or smile back this time. She's one of the good ones. She's always out in her yard doing something with her flowers or sweeping her stoop when I'm walking home from school. She always sees me and smiles.

One day we had a yard sale, I was eleven or twelve at the time. Pretty little blonde girls came with their mothers to look over all our stuff, sizing it all up, sizing us up. They looked down on us all year long, and then they came to our sale and tried to break Mama's spirit by offering a quarter when she'd marked it for a dollar.

Mama sold so many of our things that day, so many

of my things. I had a favorite shirt, a shirt from my childhood. Mama had lovingly embroidered blue and green flowers around the scooped neck and along the puffy sleeves. I couldn't keep it; it didn't fit me anymore, but I loved that shirt. A woman bought it for her little girl. What I wouldn't give to have that shirt again—to have Mama's needlework in my hands again. I'd give a lot more than a stupid quarter. Mama has no time to embroider anymore.

I'm nearing town now, the food smells and exhaust fumes come thick and fast. I want to slow down but I don't know where to go. My footfalls landing on the pavement feel hard now, jarring me. It is time to stop. I turn another corner and find myself approaching a familiar churchyard, St. Clare of Assisi hovers over me. Her stone face is patient, and there is kindness behind those unseeing eyes. Then I remember the stories about her. She ran, too, not from anything but to something.

I yank open the door and step into the cool darkness. Without bothering with the holy water or doing the sign of the cross, I run right up the aisle toward the altar. I don't think God will mind just this once. Mama would, but she's not here.

I press my palms onto the altar and collapse against it, breathing hard. My chest burns. My heart feels like it's going to explode.

St. Clare is in here, too, a smaller version to the right of center. Mother Mary is on the left and the Crucified Christ is hanging in the middle. My breathing slows. All of a sudden, I feel like they can see me—my face all sweaty and dirty, my hair all gross—and I am ashamed. I look down and study the candles on the altar, with their flickering, gold light casting moving shadows across the feet of the statues.

What am I doing here? Where am I going? What am I expecting to find here? Should I pray for the world to become a kinder, gentler place? For everyone to say they are sorry and be nice to me from now on? For the bullying girls and the grabbing boys and the dead cats of the world to all go away? For a knight to swoop in and rescue me from my life?

The open Bible is in front of me. My eyes, full of tears, snatch at a few words.

> "…the day you were born…neither washed with water nor anointed…
>
> No one looked on you with pity or compassion…you were thrown out
>
> on the ground as something loathsome, the day you were born." *

*Thrown on the ground, left to die in the muck.*

*Running amuck. There it is.*

A curse comes to my mind as the unbidden tears fall, but I dare not speak such words in church. I bite my lips in an effort to stop the curse and the tears. The words are swimming now as I read on.

"Then I passed by and saw you
weltering in your blood. I said to you:
Live in your blood and grow…"

*Live in your blood. Yep, you're stuck with it. Your blood. Your brown, Mexican blood. Your kin. The blood on your hands. Whether you did anything or not.* I read some more.

"…you came to the age of puberty;
your breasts were formed,
your hair had grown, but
you were still stark naked."

*Oh God, what is this? Is this in the Bible? Not here, too, Lord?*

My nose drips and I swipe at it with the back of my arm. I don't know if I want to keep reading or not. Maybe I should just run out of here, but I am too tired to run. I am tired of running.

"Again I passed by you and saw that
you were now old enough for love.
So I spread the corner of my cloak

over you to cover your nakedness;

I swore an oath to you and

entered into a covenant with you;

you became mine, says the Lord GOD."

*Cover you, swore an oath to you, entered into a covenant with you, and you became...*

I grip the two sides of the book and squint my eyes in the candle light. Slowing down, I deliberately read each word again.

"...you became mine, says the Lord GOD.

Then I bathed you with water,

washed away your blood, and anointed you with oil. I clothed you with

an embroidered gown..."

*Washed away your blood...an embroidered...gown.*

Suddenly I can't breathe and it's not because of the run.

"I put sandals of fine leather on your feet;

I gave you a fine linen sash

and silk robes to wear. I adorned you with jewelry...your garments were of fine linen,

silk, and embroidered cloth.

Fine flour, honey, and oil were your food."

*Flour, honey, and oil—like Mama's tortillas.* I close

my eyes and take a deep breath. I can almost taste them, almost smell her presence here with me.

"You were exceedingly beautiful,

with the dignity of a queen."

*Exceedingly beautiful. With dignity. Like a queen.*

"Magdalena?"

I stop reading and turn around. I cannot speak so I just look, holding the face with my eyes.

"The school…called me. I knew…" She chokes on her tears and swallows hard.

*How could she know? How could she know I would come here? I didn't even know.*

I keep looking at Mama with her frizzy brown hair. The pins are trying to escape from the bun. The corners of her coffee-colored eyes are creased like a fan that's been folded wrong too many times. Her lips thinned by age, tremble the slightest bit as we size one another up.

*Beautiful. With dignity. Like a queen.*

I run to her, throwing my arms around her shoulders. She hugs me hard. So hard I can't breathe. So hard I can't run away. She doesn't need to worry. I am through running.

I pull my cheek from her hair and look up at St. Clare, the Blessed Mother, and Christ Crucified. I think they can see me. I look down at the open Bible on the altar behind me. I know *He* sees me.

*Like a queen.*

(*Excerpts from Ezekiel Chapter 16, New American Bible)

# Confidence

"So I made some banana bread today," croaked a cheerful voice from the lockers behind me. "It sure did bring back memories, let me tell you."

I waited to hear someone answer her. Little old ladies don't talk on their cell phones in the locker room, do they? She probably doesn't even know what an iPhone is, right?

"I haven't made it in years, you know. Not since the kids grew up and left the house."

What..? Was she talking to me? It kind of creeped me out, so I kept digging through my bag.

"I put chocolate chips in mine. Do you like yours that way?" Stealing a glance, I spied her on the bench behind me—the little old lady with short gray curls, wrinkles all over her face, and her breasts sagging to her…

Ack! I turned back to my own locker and squeezed my eyes shut. Naked! Why is this lady naked? I mean, of course she's naked; she's in the locker room, isn't she? So there's like a fifty-fifty chance a body would be naked in here, right? But why is she talking to me? Why do sixteen year olds have to go in the *women's* locker room? In the *girls'* locker room no one talks to you. No one *naked* talks to anybody. This was so weird and I didn't know what to do. I mean, it's not like I want to be rude, right?

"I put chocolate chips in mine. Do you like yours that way?"

"Wh-what?" I tried to be polite without really looking at her.

"In my banana bread—I put chocolate chips in it. It's so good that way."

Is she still talking about banana bread? What's up with that? So funny—here I was in a towel, trying to be stealth about pulling clothes on while still being under my towel, and she's talking to me about banana bread. In the girls' locker room there were plenty of booths with curtains—for the shy girls—but in here, the curtained rooms were all full—probably with saggy ladies from the swim aerobics class.

I didn't want to hurt this lady's feelings; she seemed so nice. I looked over just as she stood up and wiggled into her big panties, beaming at me.

"Chocolate chips are good in everything," I managed. That tickled her I guess, because she just started laughing in this funny way. Tittering, I would call it, like you would expect a little old lady to laugh in a cartoon. I tried not to see how her breasts were draped over her belly or how the skin hung over her elbows and knees, like my mother's kitchen curtains. I mean I saw it, but it's not like I was looking. I didn't want to be rude.

"I saw a movie all about chocolate not too long ago," she said. "Hot chocolate and candy chocolates—it had that pirate fellow in it —what's his name?"

"Johnny Depp?" I said, surprised she would know anything about a pop culture icon like that, even if he's like, what, forty?

"That's the one. Boy, he's a looker, isn't he?" She leaned over to wink at me. Then she elbowed me, and the skin on the back of her arm flapped back and forth like a wing. She didn't even notice I was still in my towel and had managed to get my jeans pulled up only to my knees.

I blushed, and she went back to getting dressed. I got my jeans on and fiddled with my bra straps under my towel.

There were other women in there, too. Like I said, all the rooms for shy ladies were full. I could see the legs and feet of women who had more sense than to stand around naked in front of God and everybody pulling clothes off and on their bodies.

There were women over by the mirrors. *Ack!* One of them was standing there blow-drying her hair—topless!

What's up with that? Oh, and she was nothing like the granny—this lady was a goddess. She was bronze and bosomy and her muscles laid in neat little rows along the backs of her arms and across the front of her stomach. She was holding the blow dryer up over her head, and her back was chiseled like a statue we would have studied in our art class. Her breasts! They were so perfect and round—I tried not to stare. She was just incredible. My own white skin, puny muscles, and puny everything will never—could never—measure up.

"I got a good deal on Rice-a-Roni this week. Had two coupons!"

Granny was talking to me again. From the corner of my eye, she appeared to be dressed now, so I turned my attention back to her as I tied my shoes. She wore a polyester blouse, the kind you'd buy at Kmart, with blue and purple flowers on it. It hung all loose and billowy like a circus tent over her lavender pants. She snapped the elastic waistband over her tummy.

"Uh-huh," I said.

"Do you use coupons? You should, you know? It will save you so much money."

"I-I'm just in high school."

"Never too soon to start a good habit, dearie. I cut them right out of the Sunday paper—been doing it for years. Soap, sugar, cat food—you can get deals on all of that. And some stores double them, you know. At my age, that really helps stretch a dollar. But it's a good idea at any age. Why, I once…"

I looked back toward the woman in the mirrors. She was dressed now. Wow! Right off the runway! A brown suede blouse wrapped around her body and gold was draped across her chest. She studied her reflection and pulled at the jacket. She turned to check out the side view and pulled some more at her clothes. Then she leaned close to the mirror to examine her eyeliner and mascara. Her violet lipstick framed her sexy pout, just like a model. Her hair was long and thick, and she had spent a lot of time straightening it and applying some expensive-looking product to make it shiny. Tall and lean in her fitted pants and heeled boots—I wondered what kind of workout time she put in each week.

Too much. I looked away and sighed. I took in my own ripped jeans, stained shoes, favorite tee-shirt I'd worn into the ground, and my sister's jacket. It would be easy to be confident if I looked like I just stepped out of a magazine—so beautiful, so together, so comfortable in my own skin.

"…I'm not really a cat person," the little old lady was saying. "I just took in this one after my friend Maribel died. She's a cute thing though and not finicky like most. I've always owned dogs. Big dogs, little dogs, had them all my life. Friendlier, don't you think? They love you no matter how bad it gets, how ornery you can be, or how late you come home. Dogs are good people. You have a dog?"

"Jenny," I said. "She's a mutt."

"Jenny? That's a good name for a dog."

The goddess walked by me with her gym bag and purse. Her profile as she turned the corner looked hard, weary. I thought I heard her sigh as she disappeared from sight.

I turned back and looked Granny up and down—the blouse over the rolls of old lady skin; the gray curls puffed out like a fro all around her head. Her ears were big. Her nose was bigger. Her teeth were straight and white. *Probably fake.* Her skin bunched and wrinkled around her knuckles and elbows. Her neck hung in folds below her chin like a ruffled skirt.

But her eyes sparkled. Her face creased like rays of light, and her eyes were twin suns, glowing and happy, as she took me in and said, "You're a sweet girl to talk to an old woman." I couldn't help but smile.

Then she patted my knee and stood up with a groan. "Time to go, dearie," she said, hoisting her gym bag to her shoulder. "I've got a date," she said.

*Of course*, I thought. "Have a good time," I called out as she wobbled out of the locker room.

After all, who wouldn't like to spend time with someone so easy to talk to, so personable and funny in her own way—someone so comfortable in her own skin?

# Marking Time

My husband had become an old man—I never noticed it before. When the gum-chewing young nurse called us back to the examining room and he didn't have the strength to stretch out on the table with the white butcher paper, it was then that I knew it. He had become an old man, and I was going to fret over it.

Selling cosmetics, they used to tell us, "Anyone can improve their face with a smile and some moisturizer." That might fool a lot of people into thinking he's younger than he is if they were just studying his face—not that I can say Gene ever did much in the way of moisturizing anything. But the hands, the hands always tell the full story. His hands showed every chore, every task, every child, every hardship—each milestone etched in the lines. Like tally marks across his knuckles.

"O-k-a-a-y," the nurse said between popping her gum between her teeth. "What seems to be your trouble?" She never raised her eyes from the chart to really look at my husband.

After a week of feeling like an elephant was sitting on his chest, Gene let me drive him to the doctor. I rarely drive when my husband's in the car; that's just not the way women of my generation do things. But I'm a careful driver, and he was too miserable to say anything about it.

"Gene's been having a hard time breathing," I answered, but the young nurse wasn't listening. My frustration threatened to spill out all over her and that pink stripe in her hair, too, but I held my temper in check and pressed on.

"He had a bad cold lasting for over a month, and then this tightness in his chest started…" My words went limp. She scribbled in the chart like she hadn't a care in the world while my husband stared at the floor, fighting for every breath.

"Why don't you hop on up here?" the nurse said, patting the butcher-papered table like she was calling a dog for a treat. I didn't know which one of us felt hotter. Although, I could feel his fever right through his shirt sleeve.

"Miss?" I said, trying not to show my exasperation, "Can you take his blood pressure from right here? I don't think he can get on that table right now."

Gene wasn't wheezing like he had been with the cold. I'd felt so grateful when the racking cough had finally stopped, but now the lack of sound in his breathing was more upsetting than the rest of it had ever been.

She looked at him, I think for the first time, and

changed her tone. "Oh sweetie, of course you can stay there for now. You just sit tight, and I'll take your blood pressure with this cuff, o-k-a-a-y?"

I had liked her indifference better.

Gene sat passively as she pushed his sleeve up and strapped on the blood pressure cuff. His dead-eyed stare into some point toward the far wall set alarm bells off in my head. The nurse's chipper, patronizing, bobble-headed, gum-chewing demeanor made my skin crawl.

I should have known it before, about my husband becoming old. I'm old after all. I don't feel old. I don't act like an old person—hobbling around, talking about my bowel movements with the ease of commenting on the weather. But I have grown old. My hair is brittle beneath the henna, and my face is etched with lines deep enough to swim in.

I felt like Methuselah's grandmother. But when the gum-chewer pushed a folded gown into my husband's arms and oozed with concern, "Now you just put this gown on and climb up on this table, o-k-a-a-y? And the doctor will be here real soon," I wanted to kick this girl and her mother-henning ways clear into next summer. But I just smiled as she left the room.

Gene was annoyed with my trying to help him change out of his clothes, but he was too weak and short of breath to shoo me away, so there I stayed, like the Spirit of God hovering over all creation, helping him out of his dressy overalls. He'd worn the dark ones without all the wear from gardening and puttering in the tool shed. Under that he'd put on his long sleeved button up white shirt and a suit jacket to top off the whole outfit. This was the closest thing to a suit I'd ever seen my husband in. On Sundays he wore ordinary dress slacks but usually left off the jacket because our church is hotter than blazes more often than not.

I'd forgotten he wore his heavy work boots, brown and scraped with use and age. I was out of breath myself by the time I got him wrestled out of those cumbersome things and had everything folded up neatly in a pile under his chair. Normally, I would have scolded Gene for wearing those boots out to the doctor's office. I would have complained the whole time trying to get those rascals loosened and the overalls down and off his stockinged feet, but he was struggling so much just sitting there, I checked my temper again and kept still about it.

Getting him up on the table took some doing, too. No matter how I finagled that little flat pillow to keep his head raised, it never did suit him. He looked so miserable and uncomfortable, and I was miserable because I couldn't do a thing about it.

Once he got situated, Gene clasped his fingers across his chest and closed his eyes. He looked like he was fixing to be buried, and seeing his chest move up and down so weakly gave me little consolation. Pulling a chair up alongside of him, I reached out to hold his hand loosely and worried my thumb over his wedding band nestled there between the wrinkles.

So many wrinkles all along the knuckle, like tally marks. There's one for the broken down truck, two for our stubborn old egg-laying hens, three for our grown-up children, four for the decades of marriage and a line across the lot of them makes five. I couldn't think what we had five of, but it would come to me.

Normally, my husband wouldn't take me holding his hand. He'd pull it away in protest and say, "Stop fooling, woman." But maybe right now with the effort of breathing, it felt a little bit good to him.

On down below the barrel chest and soft tummy, his legs poked out from under the gown like chicken legs. They had once displayed long lean muscles from running track and chasing kids. Now they were knobby and bony.

Seeing him lying there, old and uncomfortable, his chalky knees and wrinkled hands endeared him to me all the more. Thinking of our life together, gratitude welled up in my chest and tightened my throat. I felt so thankful for all those tally marks. Here, marked out on his body, was our forty years of marriage, not like a tattoo or a scar you might hide away beneath a shirt or a pair of pants, but out in the open, like God's way of marking the days and times of our life together, the proof of our love etched there across his fingers.

One, for his shy, dimpled smile that first caught my eye back in high school. It was another girl at that time with raven locks and an easy laugh that brought out the dimple in the boy I knew—the boy before the man. In those days, I dared never speak of my feelings, I didn't really know them myself. I just knew that dimple tugged at me somewhere in the pit of my stomach or maybe in the small of my back, and I liked it. I waited to see that dimpled smile every chance I got, even if it wasn't directed at me.

Two, for the two years I admired him and he never even knew my name. We sat on the same side at church, Gene's family in the pew in front of mine. From there I could admire him and his dimple, and no one would ever have to know what I thought. It didn't matter then, the waiting. I had learned patience being the oldest girl in a family of six. Two years I watched and studied him. Two years I waited and bided my time. Two years and then I graduated from high school, and Gene came to the church's reception for all the seniors. That's when it happened. He saw me and smiled, and the dimple was mine forevermore.

Three, for three little words. Not just "I love you" or "you were right" like the saying goes. No, my husband had a habit around the house—Gene never spoke more than three words at a time about any topic when he was at home with the family. At work, in church, or while chatting up the attendant at the gas station, he could carry on with the best of them, swapping stories, telling fish tales, but at home, he mostly listened and grunted and occasionally spoke, only with three little words.

At our wedding, it wasn't "I do," but "Yes sir, preacher."

And whenever I delivered a new baby, he'd kiss my forehead and say, "You done good" or "I'm mighty proud."

While standing over him as he repaired the kitchen sink, he'd gesture loosely toward the tool box and say to me, "Sweetie, fetch that..." And I'd retrieve whatever tool he meant.

When I'd tried experimenting with some new recipe from the magazines that turned out to be wretched, the kids would all fuss and squirm, and my face would get red and my throat tight. Gene would wink and come out with his three little words—"I'll take seconds,"—and everything would be right with the world again.

Many a time he had to reprimand our children with one beefy hand firmly planted on each shoulder. He'd cock his head, look him dead in the eye and say, "Never again, hear?" The kids respected his firm but gentle reprimand, and most of the time they learned from their mistakes without repeating them.

I've always thought his reserved way showed his contentment with our family and our home. He didn't have to explain himself, defend his ways, make excuses or sell us on an idea. He said only what needed to be said with that voice that sounded like a brown sugar bear, that voice like you'd expect Abraham Lincoln's voice to be, that voice little boys use in school plays to be the grandfather or the president of the United States. His three little words said, *this is the way it is and that's all there is to it*. And the world was a nicer place to be in that moment.

Our nurse returned with some oxygen and set it up. Gene's eyes protested but nothing else could, so she slipped the tube beneath his nose anyway and promised with her patronizing pats and furrowed looks of concern that the doctor would be with us in just a few minutes.

He closed his eyes again, his breaths remaining shallow.

Oh, how I loved this man, my true love. Behind the mask of manliness and busyness, behind the tyranny of pride and authority, beneath the show and shuffle of youth and middle age, this quiet, gentle, restful giant was my husband, and I loved him dearly.

Time and life, having had its way with him, carved deep lines in his hands. I found myself wanting to stay there a while with my mind and my fingertips.

Four, I continued to tally, was for the grandchildren. Three rough and ready boys and one precious little girl who could hold her own on any climbing rope or in any ball game with the rest of them. Those four little rascals brought the dimple out in old Granddaddy Gene, and the thought of it made me smile.

There had been harsh days and heavy realities between us, too. But the lean years in our pocketbooks and in our love were all gone and forgotten now. A softness developed between us and a wonderful tenderness had grown in my husband. I didn't recognize it immediately, but when I did, I knew it was the very thing I'd longed to be *to* him and find *in* him since the day we married, since the day we met, and for all the days before I ever knew him. When I was hovering over my dolls, playing house, and wishing to be married someday, that tenderness is what I thought marriage was all about.

It was there now and had been for a while. I hadn't thought about it or about him growing so old. He squeezed my hand tightly right then, as if he were reading my thoughts.

Five, five strong fingers that still held onto mine, five fingers that held my heart. I stood up, looked into his face, and stroked his hair away from his forehead. His eyes were full, his gaze was steady.

"Our life together," I started, but the door swung open and the doctor came in with his nurse and began to give orders about taking oxygen and watching his blood pressure. Everything was going to be fine, blah, blah, blah. He was in and out quickly, but I was still caught up in my husband's gaze, holding me like it had all those years ago in church.

I helped him back on with his clothes and his boots, we stood to go, and I tried to find my words again.

"Our life together," I said again.

My husband struggled to lift his hand, the one with all those tally marks. He cupped my cheek and inhaled deeply. I saw that dimple again as he winked and said, "I'd take seconds."

# Something Out There

"Wake up!" She coughs into my face. "Gabby, wake up! Gabby…" Grams has been up smoking cigarettes in the dark, and now that putrescence is all over me.

"Gah! What is it? Stop shaking me, Grams, go away!" I pull the pillow down hard over my face and curl my legs up toward my chest. The sheet has collected around my middle and my legs are exposed to the slightest breeze coming through my window.

"Wake up, honey, I heard something! There's something out there!"

"What the heck, Grams? I'm so tired!"

"Some kind of clicking, scratching sound. Go check it out."

I lift the pillow a few inches off my face and squint at the fat glowing numbers next to my head.

"Are you out of your mind? It's the middle of the night! It's freezing cold outside!" It isn't. It's the middle of summer, but it's hard to think of a better excuse, coming out of a dead sleep like that.

She's just staring at me, mouth agape. Raising the

level of my annoyance, I try again with the excuses.

"There are freaks outside! Robbers! Grams, I'm only twelve years old, for crying out loud!"

"There it is again! Hear it? In the living room!"

*Crap! I hear it!* It's kind of a scratchy, scraping, hollow…What is that?

"Someone's ransacking the house! Hurry, Gab, hurry!"

I sit up angrily and hiss, "And what do you want me to do about it, Grams? I'm just a kid."

"Gabby, get up right now!" She's screaming at me in a whisper, if that's possible. I duck back under the pillow and wait for her to go away.

Silence.

"I think they've gone," Grams says. "Would you go check?"

I throw back the pillow and stare hard at my grandmother. She's seventy-something, I think, but she's always looked old to me. Her gray hair flies around her face like it's got a mind of its own. Her gray eyebrows stick straight out, like claws curled up over her deep-set eyes and chiseled cheekbones. Right now her lips are curling back into her mouth like she's been eating her own face; I know she keeps her teeth in the pocket of her housecoat for easy access. Yep, despite the noises of unknown origin happening somewhere in the nether-world of my house, I can definitely, in this moment, in this moon-light, know for certain that Grams is the scariest thing in this house!

I sigh and sit up. *Safer there than here.*

Getting out of bed, I creep into the hall, and Grams closes the door behind me, a little too quickly. I want to protest, but I do not want to make any more noise than we have already. I do not want to alert the *somebody* or the *something* that I'm out here and onto them.

The hallway is darker than my room. There is moon-light up ahead coming through the living room window, shining on the darkened TV. It does not reassure me.

I collapse back against my bedroom door and strain to see two feet ahead of me. My breathing is fast and loud in my ears. I make a conscious effort to slow it down.

*Breathe in, breathe out, breathe in…breathe…out.*

I long to rub my eyes and face, but I don't want to make any sudden movements so I just stare straight ahead and breathe.

To the left is Grams' room. Through the open door, I can see her yellowed sheets with the faded pansies all crumpled up on her bed. Her room is the only one in the house with a lock on the inside of it.

*A fat lot of good that did her.* It's so unfair; if I had

that lock, I wouldn't be in this mess.

Manny's room is next to hers. My little brother—he's eight. He's a good kid, quiet. He has way more patience with Grams than I do. It's like no matter how much abuse you pour on that kid, he keeps getting up. Like a dog that still loves you even when it's been getting kicked.

Grams isn't really so bad. She's just a screamer. And a sitter. She sits and smokes and watches TV all day and when we get home, she sits and smokes and gives orders all night.

She screams for stuff like slamming the door or leaving toys out or brushing our teeth too long or not getting dinner on the table fast enough. It gets old.

On the wall in front of me between the bathroom and the living room is our family photo gallery, such as it is. Those pictures have hung there for as long as I can remember. I forget about them most of the time. It's like once they're hung up, you don't look at them anymore.

There are a few dorky school pictures of Manny and me. I stopped getting those when I hit middle school.

An old black and white one of Grams hangs on a wire. She was in high school or something—before she married, before she had any kids.

My favorite is of Manny and I under the Christmas

tree when I was, like, four and Manny was just able to sit up without toppling over.

My parents divorced that year.

We had the biggest Christmas ever that year.

There's one of Grams standing next to the neighbor's old Ford Mustang. He had spent years fixing it up, and he was so proud. Manny is behind the wheel, wearing sunglasses and pretending to drive.

I was in Germany that summer, where Dad lives. He took me on a palace tour in Ludwigsburg and I got to dress up like a princess; it was cool, like a fairytale. I wish I had a picture of that on the wall.

Dad didn't send for Manny that year, and I haven't seen him since then either.

The picture at the end of the hall is of me in roller skates holding our kitten. It was taken when I was ten. That was the year I stopped believing in the tooth fairy and the Easter bunny. The kitten got into trouble with Grams, and she gave it away one day while I was at school. I had hoped in those days, that if I was really good, …

I had hope in those days.

I can't really make out any of the pictures in the dark with their mismatched frames, but I know in this one with the roller skates, there is an apple tree in the background. That was our old house, our old backyard. My mom's hand is in the foreground, reaching out to steady me on my skates. Mom's arm in her army fatigues. Mom. Mom.

*Dead.* That thought comes out of nowhere, sliding off the wall from somewhere behind me, slithering through my ear, creeping into my consciousness, and making me shiver like no cool breeze ever could. My mom, Elizabeth Maren Scott, dead at age thirty-six…only she isn't really dead. Just dead to me. Dead to me.

Other kids' moms and dads join the military because they were drafted or their parents made them do it or they needed money for college or they're just really patriotic. They go off and serve somewhere in Europe or Asia or Iraq or wherever. They either die over there, heroes to the world, or they come home again to be with their kids and their wives and husbands—heroes to their families, back to make a home together…forever.

My mom joined the army for no good reason, as far as I can tell. No one made her do it. She didn't need the money. She just went.

And she did not go off to Iraq. She did not go off to die. She got stationed in New Mexico—or somewhere not too far from here—and just decided not to take us with her. She left us here with Grams. She left us here.

She left me.

*What's so special? What's so special that you would leave us for wherever, whoever...*

A girl in my class, Monique, she has a mom like mine, only she's not in the army. She's in a relationship. She's *always* in a relationship, first with one guy and then with another.

Yeah, this girl has three younger brothers and sisters to take care of. *Halfs,* she calls them, all with different daddies. Monique hates it. She's not really a friend, but she sits at my lunch table, complaining about her life and begging chips and cookies off the rest of us.

They get theirs first, she says, her little brothers and sisters. She gets their supper fixed, they eat, and if there is any leftover, she gets it. Sometimes she's just too tired to eat. Her mom is always out on a date, or sometimes (worse), she stays at home, behind closed doors, on a date.

Maybe Monique's just a drama queen and she just made it all up, I don't know. I don't say much to her, but I think I believe her. I try not to think about her mom. Or mine.

Monique's mom must do it for the same reason my

mom did it. I don't know what that reason is but there's something out there—something taking her time and touching her heart more than I do.

I turn around and open my door slowly. I don't know how long I was out there. Grams is still standing rigid and frightened, hovering over my bed in the moonlight.

"I don't hear it anymore. I'm going back to bed." I crawl back in the sheets and turn my back to her. I can feel she is still there. I don't tell her that I never left the hallway. What she don't know…

\*\*\*\*\*\*\*\*\*\*\*

"Gabs, Gabs! There's something out there! It's outside now!"

Aargghh! What am I gonna do with her? I've got to get some sleep for school tomorrow.

"Grams!" I snap, "leave me alo…" Then I get a good look at her and even in the darkness I can see…

"What are you doing with your gun out?! Grand-mother! Put that thing away! You're scaring the crap outta me!"

"Gabby, take this outside and check again. I swe…"

"Grams, it's only been twenty minutes! Did you ever even *leave* my room? Have you just been standing there in the dark like an old witch?!"

"Gabby! Of course I left!" she bellows. She looks even more ominous now, if that's possible. Waving the gun around, her Medusa mop of hair flops around. Her bloodshot eyes look like they're going to pop out and roll under my bed. Her exposed knees, like wrinkly door knobs, wobble on skinny white legs. Her torn house dress hangs woppy-jawed off one shoulder.

I swear, if *she* would just go out there herself, she'd scare whatever it was far away from this house and they'd never come back.

"Now stop fussing and get out of this bed, Gabriella!"

*Oh crap, she's using my full name now.* I sit up and try to put on a patient face, I can still hear the screech of irritation in my voice. "I'm telling you, Gram's there's nothing out there."

"And I'm telling you to go outside and check or I'm going to turn you over my knee." I try not to laugh.

"You're not too big for that, you know. I'm still boss around here, young lady, and…"

"I'm up, I'm up." I slide out of bed, dragging the sheet to the floor behind me. It's starting to get colder in my room. I'm so sleepy.

"Here, take the…"

"I'm not taking the gun! Forget it!"

The living room seems less scary now. Too tired to

care, I practically march toward the light, daring anything or anyone to come and find me. I turn right and stop.

The front room looks normal. The couch sags. The air is stale. The TV is dark. The coffee table is full of Gram's crap—overflowing ash trays and the remotes for the TV and VCR. I jiggle the front door knob to see if it's locked.

"Gabs?"

"Aaaaaaahh!" I scream and reach for the door. I fumble to unlock it, whip open the screen and leap off the porch into the grass. I think I twisted my ankle but I don't have time to think about it. I limp for cover behind our neighbors' trash cans on the curb and duck down holding my breath.

*What was that? Who is in my house? Oh God, if you're up there...*

I peek out and squint toward the porch. The screen is wide open, but the hard door is closed. Then I see Grams standing in the window, holding back the curtain and staring into the darkness.

*Crap! It was her!* I march up the front walk and stomp up the steps.

"Grams! Grams! You scared the crap out of me! What were you thin...Grams! Grams? Unlock this door!!" I pound on the door with my fist. My ankle hurts.

"What the heck—you locking me outside? What're you thinking? There's nothing out here!!"

Grams unlocks the door, but she doesn't look convinced. I am madder than I have ever been. "What if there were bad guys out there and you locked the door like that—your only granddaughter trapped out there only in my pajamas and at somebody's mercy! Sheesh, Grams! What were you thinking?!"

"Alright, alright, stop your bellyaching, Gabby, I'm right here."

I am breathing so hard. I'm so angry I could spit. My skin feels cold in the night air, but little needles are shooting up through my feet and into my legs, making me hot, hotter than I ever thought I could be.

Grams cowers next to me. She looks small and embarrassed and apologetic. Her wild hair looks limp. Her face and shoulders sag like the couch and the room.

I sigh.

"I'm okay, Grams. We're okay."

"Okay? Good." She says meekly. Then regaining her confidence she straightens and says, "Now, in case they come back…"

"Who's coming back?! Who, Grams? Nobody's out there!"

'Yeah, I know, but in case they come back..."

"Grandmother!" I feel like the parent now, like I'm the adult.

"In case the NOISE comes back," she lifts up her gun to show me.

"Grams!" I scold her again.

Stepping around her and over to the couch, I drop down into the cushion and bury my face in my hands. I can't believe Manny is sleeping through all this. And the dogs? They haven't been barking at all. If there had really been somebody in the house, wouldn't they be howling in the garage, barking and carrying on? Surely they'd be letting us know.

"You pull back this thingy on top, then pull the trigger under here."

I'm too exasperated to shout anymore. "Grams, I'm not shooting that thing! I'm twelve! I'll probably shoot my own foot off or get hauled off by the cops or something!"

"Are you refusing to obey me, little girl? Are you saying no to your grandmother? After all I've done for..."

I'm so tired. "Okay, Grams. Enough."

I look at her. She's so tiny, shriveled. I sigh again. "What do I have to do?"

"You sit here on the couch and keep watch."

"Keep watch?"

"Keep watch…with the gun."

"With the gun?"

"I could get your brother to do it?"

"Manny is eight!"

"Every boy's gotta grow up sometime. He'll be man of the house soon enough, I should think."

"You're right, Grams," I drip, "he's practically an adult."

"Somebody's got to be."

I look at her, incredulous. "Look who's talking—Grand-mother!"

"Act your age, young lady!!"

"ACT YOURS, GRAMS!!!"

"Gabriella, how can you take that tone with me!? You're going to make me cry."

I feel sorry despite myself. "Look, don't let loose on me, will ya?" I take a deep breath and let it out slowly. "Tell me again, which thingy do I pull first?"

She wipes her nose with the back of her hand and sniffles. "The one on the top. Oh, you'll do fine, Gabby, I know you will."

"Thanks."

"And if we're still alive in the morning, I'll make your favorite chocolate chip waffles."

"*If* we're still alive."

"You're a good girl, Gabby."

"Yeah, Grams, I know."

\*\*\*\*\*\*\*\*\*\*\*\*\*

When I open my eyes again, it's morning. The gun is on the floor at my feet. The sun is streaming onto the coffee table. I am not sure how much sleep I've gotten, but I don't feel as tired as you would think. I'm surprised to find a crocheted afghan across my body.

Manny is awake, sitting on the floor in his pajamas, watching cartoons.

"Morning, Gabby."

"Hi Manny."

"I got my own breakfast," he says.

"I see that." Little cereal circles and squares are sprinkled around him like confetti.

"Did you let the dogs out yet?"

"Grams did it," he says, "and guess what?"

"What?" I say, sleepily.

"Those crazy dogs knocked over the trash cans in the garage and ate up half our trash last night."

"Really?" I say.

"Yeah, Grams thinks it was the pizza box they were after. It's a mess out there. I didn't touch it though.

Grams said when you got up…"

*Oh, goodie.* I close my eyes and squeeze my toes, up and down. There's something out there alright, and I get to clean it up. I better get off my butt; Grams will be screaming for me to get off her spot any minute now. Anyway, I hope there's chocolate chip waffles for breakfast.

I hope.

# The Real Deal

"So, it says here he was born on June 9, 1963 in Owens-boro, Kentucky. That was twenty-six years ago." The two girls laid side-by-side, propped up on their elbows, sur-rounded by pink throw pillows and stuffed animals, with the latest copy of *Dream Teen* magazine open between them. *Simple Minds* sang from a ghetto blaster perched on the open window.

"So?"

"So?" Twelve-year-old Laura Nicole Justice rolled her hazel eyes as if the strain of explaining everything to her best friend Gina was exhausting to her. "June ninth is my mom's birthday! And she met *my dad* in Kentucky when she was in law school. It fits!"

"What fits? So what if your mom and Johnny Depp have the same birthday? That doesn't mean he's your long lost brother."

Laura had been best friends with Gina Riordan since the third grade when the super-pretty, never-shy-new-girl invited herself to sit at Laura's lunch table on the first day, and they'd been inseparable ever since. Even then, Gina's good looks intimidated Laura, though she had never dared voice that anywhere except in her diary. While Laura was short for her age and unhappily still lacking any curves, Gina's long legs and crazy-thick hair made her look more like one of Charlie's Angels than a soon-to-be seventh-grader at Andrew Jackson Junior High.

Laura's mom had tried to help her feel a little more feminine by giving her a home perm the weekend before sixth grade graduation.

"What do you think, sweetheart?" her mother had asked, placing a small hand mirror in front of her only daughter, quivering with excitement.

Mom! What did you do?"

"I think it's sweet on you."

"I think I'm hideous."

"Call Gina over," her mom said, trying not to sound hurt, "see what she thinks about it."

"She'll say I look like a French poodle."

Gina had ridden over, thrown her bike down in the yard, and run through the back door without even knocking.

"Ack! You look like a French poodle," she spat out before seeing the hurt in Laura's eyes. Then she amended, "But not in a bad way."

Having tried and failed to fix her best friend's new

hairdo with a pair of sewing scissors later that day, Gina lent Laura a colorful array of headbands to wear for the summer until her hair grew out again. Her efforts did little to boost Laura's hopes of becoming cool before the start of junior high, so Laura had written off the hair issue and turned her sights to deeper, more serious matters. She wrote about them in her diary every day that summer, including "the hidden truth secreted away my whole life by my parents which, when uncovered, will inevitably change my destiny forever."

Now Laura was not so sure it had been a good idea to share her thoughts with her best friend. But for the sake of their friendship, she put on her patient face and kept trying. "Long lost *half*-brother."

"Half-brother?" Gina said. "And *you* have *half* a brain!"

"Haven't you ever noticed that lots of people have birthdays that are the same as other members of their family? I think it has something to do with the hormones."

"Hormones? What do you know about hormones?"

"Gina, if you expect to get anywhere in life you'll have to start reading something besides fashion magazines and *Teen Beat*."

"What else is there?" Gina retorted.

"Hello—*National Geographic, The New Yorker, Psychology Today.*"

"Shut up!" Gina said, smacking her friend on the back of the head with a heart pillow. "You and your *Psychology Today.*"

"I know what I know," Laura said. "So—maybe there's a lot more hormones in…June, May, April," she counted backwards on her fingers, "September. My mom must have gotten pregnant in September to have a baby in June."

"Ew, gross! I don't want to think about your mom getting *pregnant.*"

"Grow up, Gina, this is important. If I can find out more of Johnny's personal history, I can prove he's my brother."

"Half-brother."

"Right." This was exhausting. Laura needed to take a breather. She rolled off the bed and moved to the window to flip the cassette tape over. Then she stood there, clutching her half of the "Best Friends Forever" charm she wore at all times, pressing the cool metal against her chin. Over the fence, she could see a boy from school mowing her neighbor's grass. She didn't know his name, but she took note that he was cute.

Gina sat up and reached for the *Pinch-Me-Pink* nail

polish on Laura's night stand. Shaking it as directed, the bottle click-clacked against her mood ring as she rolled it between her palms. Placing her right foot over a well-worn copy of *Are You There God? It's Me, Margaret,* she painted all the toenails of her right foot and sighed heavily when she saw how much of it got on the surrounding skin.

Turning from watching the boy next door, Laura looked at her friend. Spying the nail polish dilemma, she dug around in her desk drawer and came up with some Q-tips and nail polish remover. Then sitting on the bed, Laura placed her friend's foot in her lap and began to remedy the sloppy edges of each toenail. This was familiar territory for both of them. Gina was no better with nail polish than she had been with the scissors, and Laura had often fixed the mess. It's what friends do.

Gina finally spoke. "So, why is this so important to you? I'm trying to understand, but truthfully, I'd rather marry the guy than find out he's my brother."

"Husbands come and go, Gina, but a brother is forever. If you had a connection, a deep, real, blood connection with somebody as special as Johnny Depp, wouldn't *you* want to know about it?

Gina switched feet so Laura could paint the other one. "I'd like to have a real deep connection with Michael

J. Fox or Kirk Cameron."

"Gina! Stay focused. You can drool later."

"Pig."

"Brat."

"Dork."

"Airhead."

"Wannabe."

"Enough," Laura said, "This is childish. Johnny's destiny is on the line."

"Destiny?" Gina scoffed. "I think Johnny's doing fine without you or anyone else interfering with his destiny."

"Doing fine? How can you say that? He's been divorced already and had two broken engagements. He doesn't need one more bimbo girlfriend wrecking his life. He needs me—a regular girl—to be a sister to him. He needs a regular family living in a regular town…"

"Eating regular junk food on a regular Saturday night with your regular best friend—I get it, I get it. You're so normal."

Laura shoved Gina's foot off her lap playfully and put the nail polish back on the night stand. "Johnny needs normal, don't you think? So are you with me, *best friend*?"

Gina studied her toes, then her friend's face. Laura's kinky hair didn't look so bad now that it had grown out a bit. Lending her some nice headbands had helped, too.

"I'm with you," Gina said. "You may be a spaz and a half, but you're *my* spaz and a half."

"I love you, too," Laura said, blowing Gina a kiss.

"Okay, what do we know so far?"

Laura reached for her diary where she had been creating a list. "Birthday: same as my mom's. Birth state: place where my parents met. Eyebrows: bushy and dark, just like mine."

"And that's a good thing?"

"Gina, focus."

Gina gave Laura a thumbs-up. Laura waggled her eyebrows in return and both girls laughed.

"So you think your mom got pregnant by some guy when she was twenty-something…"

"She would have been nineteen. That fits."

"Can you imagine? What if you get pregnant when you're nineteen? She would totally freak!"

"Totally."

"So, you think she gave Baby Johnny up for adoption?"

"Right."

"Stuck around long enough to meet *your* dad?"

"Stuck around in the same state, but not in the same town. My mom met my dad playing ping pong with the soldiers at Fort Campbell. But Johnny was born in Owensboro."

"I wonder how far away they are from each other," Gina said.

"Only a couple of hours maybe."

The girls sat still for a minute, staring at one another.

"You know what we've got to do, Gina?"

"Uh-huh. Let's get the bikes."

The two girls scrambled off Laura's bed and slipped into their sandals. Downstairs, Laura grabbed two pudding pops from the freezer and called to her mom that they were going for a bike ride.

"Where you girls headed?"

"The library," they said in unison.

"Check back in an hour."

"Okay. Love ya."

"Love you. See ya, Gina."

"Bye, Mrs. Justice. Thanks for the pudding pop."

"No problem."

Ugly and square, Jackson Public Library had been erected back in the late sixties next to the White Horse Funeral Parlor. Though very uninviting for most teenagers, Laura and Gina knew the place by heart. They parked their bikes out front and headed straight for the microfiche located downstairs.

Sliding the plastic card around under the magnifier, Gina took care to find what her friend was so desperate to know. "Aha, here's something," she said. "It says here that Johnny's mom is a waitress, and his dad is a civil engineer."

"A waitress? Why would a big shot engineer marry a waitress? That doesn't add up."

"You might be right. It also says his parents divorced when he was fifteen."

"Wow! Right in the middle of his impressionable teenage years," Laura said. "That's so bogus!"

"I guess they tried to make the most of it, but they just weren't meant to be."

"Does it show a picture of his parents?"

"No, why?"

"Just thinking..." Laura squinted pensively, focusing on the far wall behind Gina's head.

"What? What?" Gina asked.

"What if my mom didn't give him up for adoption to a couple of strangers," Laura said, her eyes widening. "What if his dad is really his dad...and then my mom couldn't keep the baby...and..."

"Wait, are you saying your mom hooked up with John Christopher, the engineer, and then ran away to pursue her career, leaving him to raise the baby alone?

Isn't that a little farfetched, Laura? What do you have against your dad anyway?"

"Nothing. My dad's great. I'm just trying to make the pieces fit."

"Just brainstorming."

"Right."

"So why wouldn't your mom have kept the baby?"

"Maybe Grandpa Willie said no."

Raising her fist to her chin, Gina leaned in and did her best Madonna impression: "And I made up my mind: I-I'm keeping my baby. Ooh! I'm gonna keep my baby."

"Get ser-i-ous!" Laura said. "No, really, maybe Grandpa and Grandma didn't know about the baby and Mom was making plans to go to law school and…"

"Do you really think your mom would get rid of her own kid? She doesn't seem like the type."

"She doesn't seem like the type to keep this big secret from everybody either."

"I don't know, Laura."

"Maybe my mom is more mysterious than any of us ever thought."

"Doo-doo-doo-doo, doo-doo-doo-doo," Gina sang the theme to *The Twilight Zone.*

"Shut up."

"This idea of yours is just so out there. Maybe you have a long lost brother or maybe you're really just a screwed-up teenager with a flair for the dramatic."

"Hey!" Laura shouted.

"Hey, yourself!"

"You're making me feel stupid!"

"Well, you're acting kind of—"

"Really? Is that what you think, that this is a big waste of time, that *I'm* a big waste of time? If I'm so stupid, why are you still here? Maybe *you're* the stupid one for being a friend with someone like me!" Laura slid down the side of the microfiche counter and buried her face in her arms.

Gina stood lamely. She hadn't meant to hurt Laura. Even if she was a screwed-up drama queen, she was her drama queen.

Gina dug out another plastic microfiche card and placed under the magnifier. After a few minutes she caught her breath. "Oh my."

"What?" Laura exclaimed, forgetting to pout. "What is it?"

Glad to have her friend back, Gina skimmed the article, "After his parents divorced, the family moved a lot...to Florida...his mom remarried...he engaged in self...self-harm?"

"Oh my goodness, are you sure?" Laura jumped up to see for herself.

"They even quoted him: '*My body is a journal in a way...you make a mark on yourself...with a knife or...*'"

"A knife?" Laura asked.

"That's what it says: '*A knife or with a tattoo artist. We're all damaged in our own way,*' he says. '*Nobody's perfect. I think we are all somewhat screwy, every single one of us.*'"

"Oh, my poor Johnny. I wish I could have been there for him."

"I wish *I* could be there for him," Gina said, "I'd like to see all those tattoos and kiss every one of his scars."

"Gina! That's my brother you're talking about! If anyone's going to comfort him, it should be family."

"Fine! Keep him all to yourself."

The girls stopped talking. The gravity of what they had learned left them without words. Laura studied the article on the microfiche, Gina looked at her pink toenails poking out of her sandals. After a minute, Laura broke the silence.

"Gina?"

"Yeah?"

"Did you ever know somebody who, you know?"

"What, cut themselves?"

"Who would do that?" Laura asked

"I don't know. Maybe somebody who was really sad."

"We're not even in the seventh grade yet. Who could be that sad?"

Gina was still studying her toes. Without looking up, she said, "Stephanie maybe."

"Stephanie that smells bad?" Laura jerked her head up and caught her friend's eye.

"Yeah," Gina said.

Laura dropped her voice to a whisper. "Stephanie that got her period when she was, like, eight?"

"Yeah."

"Stephanie—what's her last name?"

"Williams," Gina said. "Stephanie Williams. She lives behind the bank where my mom works."

"You think she does it?"

"Does what?"

"It."

"*It*-it or *cuts herself-it*?"

"Cuts herself, like Johnny."

"I don't know, maybe. She always looks so sad and alone. I mean, if I was her, I might, you know."

Laura's eyes widened, her face reddening with shame.

"Have you ever talked to her?"

"No, have you?"

"No."

Laura wondered if her friend felt as bad as she did about Stephanie. She knew she would have to go home and write about it in her diary, but she couldn't think about it anymore at the moment. She changed the subject.

"I've got to find him, Gina. You see how he is. So awkward and shy and looking for acceptance. I've got to let him know that somebody out there really loves him, not like all those stupid girl-crushes but loves him for keeps."

"Well, he's got other brothers and sisters, you know."

"Yeah, but I'm more than blood. I'm the real deal," Laura said.

"You *think* you're the real deal."

The librarian walked by the girls with an armful of books. The girls blushed. Laura picked up her *Best Friends Forever* charm and chewed on it nervously.

"Laura?

"What?"

"Johnny Depp feels like crap a lot, right?"

"Right."

"He said that no matter how famous he gets and how many people go and see his movies, he still has no real hope, right?"

"That's why I want to help him. That's why I…"

"Laura, let's be real. No matter what letters you write with whatever proof you've collected, he's never gonna know about it. His agents or fan club or whoever, they're the ones that get all that stuff. You know they're just gonna throw it away along with all the stalker mail."

Laura sighed, "I know." She hated to admit Gina was right. Gina with the perfect hair and perfect legs. Gina who'd never been shy or awkward or uncomfortable about anything for as long as she had known her. Next to her, Laura had nothing—no looks, no class. And if the Johnny-thing turned out to be a fluke, she'd have no special secret. She'd have to think of some new, important thing to give her life meaning.

Gina looked up at the clock on the wall. "We better get back. You're mom's going to wonder what happened to us."

"Yeah," Laura said, trying not to show her disappointment.

The girls returned the books and microfiche, thanked the librarian and headed for the bike racks out front. Laura chewed on her charm.

"Hey, what's still eating you?" Gina asked.

Laura didn't answer right away. She wasn't sure she even knew what she was thinking. She kept nibbling at the charm and walking toward her bike. When they arrived at the bike rack, her face brightened.

"You know what you said about Stephanie?"

"Yeah," Gina said, fiddling with her bike lock.

"She could use a real friend."

"Yeah."

"Let's do it, Gina." Laura was excited. She pulled her head band off, ruffled her hair and placed the head band on purposefully. "Let's totally take her on. It'll be like a pet project. We could sit next to her at lunch and help her with her hair."

"Makeover—Laura, I love it! I'll get my mom's scissors."

"Oh, like you did for me?"

"It could have worked. Your hair's just weird."

"Thanks," Laura said, twirling the streamers on her handlebars between her fingers. She had been meaning to cut them off all summer, but she just couldn't bring herself to do it yet.

"It's probably just hormones," Gina teased.

"Shut up!"

"You shut up!"

The girls moved out toward the street, walk-riding slowly until they had to part ways.

"Do you really need Johnny when you've got me?"

Gina asked. "Friends can be the real deal, too, ya know."

Laura smiled.

"I mean, who else would go on this wild goose chase with you?"

"Yeah."

"And let you keep Johnny for yourself even though I could be really good for him, too, and not in a bad way."

"Yeah."

"Call me later?"

"Okay, but only after *21 Jump Street* is over."

"Do you think you'll confront your mom about her mysterious past?"

"I don't know. I hope she doesn't wig out."

"As if! Your mom's so cool."

"Yeah, I know." The girls walked silently for a moment.

"Gina?"

"Yeah?"

"Thanks."

"What are friends for, right?" Gina blew a kiss and rode toward her house.

Laura scooted back on the banana seat of her bike and pedaled in the other direction. Thinking of Gina's friendship, her mom's mysterious past, Johnny Depp's confession of cutting, and the possibility of befriending

Stephanie Williams when she started back to school in the fall—Laura smiled all the way home. She had such a long *to-do* list to write up in her diary, and the summer was almost over.

# Unwelcome Guest

"Why are you here?" I said irritably, flipping on the kitchen light and squinting at my unwelcome visitor. A tall blonde sat at my kitchen table in a smart black pencil skirt and heels. Her upswept hair and neat make-up made me feel even frumpier and dumpier in my over-sized robe and dishwater hair pulled back in a scrunchie.

"It's barely six in the morning," I said, gulping back the bile that sprang up in the pit of my stomach.

Studying me up and down, she said soberly, "Would you believe God sent me?"

"Ha ha," I deadpanned. Inwardly I hoped she wasn't right.

On the way to the coffee maker, I smelled last night's spaghetti dishes piled up in the sink and gagged at the day-old tomato sauce and grease hanging in the air. I dreaded having to face that saucepan later with a scrubber, but I doubted I could get one of the kids to do it for me.

"Coffee?" I asked, not really meaning it.

My visitor snorted and shook her head.

"So what brings you here so bright and early?" I asked. For a moment I considered dumping the old coffee grounds in her lap, but thinking better of it, I dumped them in one of my neglected houseplants instead. It wouldn't do much good, but I poked the grounds down into the dried out soil anyway using a broken chop stick I had found on the counter. Like me, the plant was brown, limp, and probably beyond repair.

As if she read my mind, she smiled, I scowled, and finished up with my coffee preparations.

"I came to lend you a hand," she chirped, all politeness and propriety. "You obviously need it. Where do you keep your planner?" She stood and began straightening the little piles that had built up on my countertops. Last month's spelling tests that hadn't made it up on the fridge yet. Utility and cell phone bills still needing to be paid. Bedraggled coloring books. Overdue library books on organization and personal success. Unheeded phone messages. Untried recipes I had clipped from the newspaper with good intentions.

"I don't keep a planner anymore," I said flatly.

"You don't keep a planner anymore?"

"Nope."

"I can't say I'm not disappointed," she said, settling back down at the table. Her smugness sent a shiver down my spine.

Shuffling through the cupboard for some cereal, my hand brushed against something sticky. It was probably syrup, but with her watching, I decided to pass on licking my hand to find out.

Working hard to ignore my guest, I poured crunchy cardboard bits into a bowl and reached for the milk. Then I searched through my piles till I found a magazine, sat down, and opened it up to an article titled "50 Ways to Say No and Feel Good Doing It."

"So what's on the agenda for today?" she asked, starting a list on the back of my son's field trip permission slip I'd forgotten to sign and return to the teacher. One heeled foot grazed my shin a little too sharply from under the table as she crossed her legs.

"I'll pass," I blurted out, biting my lip against the pain.

"Supper for six," she narrated, "which is healthy, economical, and beautifully presented. Something your husband will actually enjoy eating and your children will…"

"Would you please shut up?" I hollered. "I'm eating. If you can call this low fat sh…stuff…food."

"Tut, tut. Using such filthy language so early in the morning. What if one of your children hears you?"

"I didn't use filthy language."

"You would have if I wasn't here."

"Shame, shame."

Sighing, I slammed down the magazine and carried my mostly full bowl of cereal to the sink to dump it out.

"Wasting food? Oh my, isn't that one of the seven deadly sins?" she asked.

Another curse word flashed through my mind. Silently, I directed it at her through furrowed eyebrows.

"You should go meditate or workout or something," she said. "You need to improve your mood."

"What's your problem?" I snapped.

"*You're* my problem, little missy. You're being ugly and rude and out of control," she said.

"If you don't like it, leave. I didn't ask you to come here." She was right about me feeling out of control, but I wasn't going to admit it to her.

"Working out is out of the question since you put your yoga mat and workout DVD back in storage."

If snarkiness was a piece of clothing, it would fit her like a glove. "I think your Bible is around here somewhere in this…"

*Mess,* I finished for her in my thoughts. We both looked hopelessly around at the piles of papers and dishes and then at each other. Unable to bear her scrutiny, I closed my eyes.

My hair felt itchy. My neck and shoulders were full of little knots, one for every painful barb she flicked my way. She's always right about me and I hate her for it. I hate me for it.

"Okay," I sighed, slouching back toward my chair, while she rummaged around gleefully, looking for my old, black, leatherbound Bible. I used to find real comfort and peace in there and made a point to read a few verses every morning before I started my day. Lately, though, I'd become so distracted, busy, and overwhelmed with *accommodating* my guest, that weariness and discouragement had become constant companions.

"Here it is, sweetie," she chirped, laying the Bible on the table in front of me. Running my fingers along the cover, my fingertips played along the pen marks and torn edges. The gold embossing that had once been my name had become lost and unrecognizable. I flipped to the middle where I had placed the bookmark months ago.

"Maybe you should pray first."

"Would you go be somewhere else please?" I said.

"Sorry," she whispered. "I'll leave you and God alone, to get…reacquainted."

I hoped she felt my eyes burning a hole into the back of her head as she tiptoed into the living room, switched on a table lamp, and settled herself onto my couch. Even from way over there, she looked smug, and I bristled.

I bowed my head, squeezed my eyes shut, and covered my head and ears with my hands in an effort to block her out.

"Lord…" I prayed.

"Wow, you call Him 'Lord?'" she asked from across the room, "but is He your *Lord*?"

Frustrated she was eavesdropping on my intimate moment, I pressed my palms more tightly into my ears and began an inner dialogue that was not very prayerful. When I had regained some composure, I began praying aloud again, attempting to refocus my thoughts. "Lord, I thank you for this day…"

"Tsk, tsk. You always say the same thing."

Willing her not to hear me, I scrunched my whole face up and blurted out quickly before she could interrupt me again:

"Lord, thank You for this day and for the breakfast and for time with You *alone* this morning. Help me tune out every voice but Yours, to grow into a deeper knowledge of You and of who You've made me to be.

"So that You will be proud of me."

"What?" I said, looking up.

"Say it. You know you want to."

"No, I don't. Stop reading my mind!" Then, so she

wouldn't hear me, I silently mouthed, "And please be proud of me." Then I finished with a shout, "Amen."

She snickered as I opened my Bible to the bookmarked page. "Psalms again?"

"Yes, Psalms again. Do you have a problem with Psalms?"

"You *always* read Psalms. You hardly go anywhere else in the Bible. Have you even read the whole Bible? Ever?"

"I've read it! I've read the whole Bible! A few times! Well, most of it, anyway." I don't know why I'm talking to her, entertaining her accusations. Why does she have such a hold on me?

She raised one eyebrow skeptically, disdain quivering from her lower lip like snake venom.

"Have you ever read *Zephaniah*?" she asked.

*Zephaniah? Is that even a book in the Bible?*

"Have you?" I challenged.

She flipped the magazine onto the coffee table and chuckled. She made an obvious show of enjoying my fumbling through the soft pages of my Bible till I finally stopped on the Table of Contents.

Flipping to Zephaniah, I skimmed through the first chapter catching a few words: *violence, deceit, wicked, destroy*. She blinked at me and waited. One tight slap would wipe that amused expression right off her self-satisfied face.

"Okay," I said, closing my Bible, "this is not helping."

"Giving up so easily?" she said, less like a question and more like a statement.

"I'm not giving up."

"You closed your Bible."

"And? I can open it again."

"Really? When?" she said, rising from the couch and walking cat-like toward the kitchen. "When the kids are up, being noisy or nosy, getting dressed or brushing teeth? Have you even made their lunches yet? Good mothers make lunches the night before, you know. Good mothers pack fruit and veggie sticks and homemade cookies.

I sat dumbly as she continued. "What about breakfast?" Menace flashed in her eyes as she sidled up to the kitchen table and towered over me in my robe and slippers. "Were you planning to make pancakes for your sweet darlings or just cereal, like you always do? Good mothers make a hot breakfast, offering a variety of healthy food choices for their children before they go off to school to learn and grow and become better little people!"

I could no longer hold her gaze.

"Are you even dressed yet?" she accused, hissing into my ear. "Did you bother to comb your hair and brush your teeth before sending your husband off to work this morning? No wonder he doesn't kiss you at the door. You're wretched! And what's with these *old lady* sweats all the time? You think that's what he wants to look at when he wakes up in the morning and when he goes to bed at night?"

I wish she would wag that witch's claw of hers just a little bit closer.

She picked up the list she had started and shook it in my face.

"What else is *always* on your list that you *never* do? Call your mother? Floss your teeth? Drink eight glasses of water!? "Did you drink your water this morning? Did you stop to think for one minute that your kidneys need a break after a long night of processing whatever crap you shoveled into them the night before, that your body is seventy percent water and it could use a glass or two of refreshment before you..."

"Stop! Stop!" I wailed. "I *am* a mess! I *am* a terrible mother! I *am* a big, fat slob, loser of a human being, and I'll never get it right even if I wanted to, even if I tried really hard, even if I made a real effort, because I'm a no good, lazy, selfish person and a miserable failure, and it's not even seven o'clock in the morning!" I stormed out of the kitchen in tears.

Reaching for the handrail by the stairs, I yelped as I felt talons dig hard into my shoulders. "Don't forget to wake your children with a cheerful *good morning,*" she jeered as I tried to catch my balance. I lunged toward the bathroom door just as she leapt onto my back, smacking my face hard against the wall.

With the wind knocked out of me, I staggered under the weight of her. Dropping to the floor, my knees cracked against the tiles.

"You never did finish reading Zephaniah this morning," she said, yanking a handful of my hair and digging her heel into the back of my leg.

"I…am not…going to…fight…you," I said, rolling over and thrusting my right elbow into her ribs. I heard a thud as her head smacked against the rim of the toilet. She howled in pain.

I managed to get on all fours and back away from her. She was holding her head, her face in a grimace.

"Do you want to know what else Zephaniah says? It says, 'What a ruin she has become…she accepts no correction, she does not trust in the LORD, she does not draw near…'"

"It doesn't say *she.*"

"It does," she purred, "and doesn't that sound just like you? Not heeding instruction? Not trusting God? Unprincipled. Treacherous. Profane. You expect to be powerful and poised and peaceful? You can't even keep a planner, read your Bible, or finish a prayer!"

"Enough," I panted. "I have had enough of you!" I leapt on her and bit down hard on her bony shoulder.

"Oooooowwwww!" she bellowed, her back falling into the door knob.

I climbed over her and out of the bathroom. Then I hurled myself down the stairs, sweat pants rippling in my wake. I snatched my Bible off the table and began shouting into the air:

"I'll show you some Bible reading, you putrid wench! I'll show you prayer and peace and power in the Lord! You want me to read Zephaniah? I'll read Zephaniah! I'll show you whose reading Zephaniah!"

My voice was a shriek, my eyes were ablaze, and the back of my head felt like it was on fire. Electricity vibrated every cell in my body as I flipped back to Zephaniah, landing in the third chapter.

"She obeys no one, she accepts no correction," I read. *Oh crap, this can't be it.* I read on.

"She does not trust in the Lord, she does not draw near to her God." *No, no, no, I will not panic. I am not that woman.* I skimmed on down:

> "The Lord within her is righteous;
>> He does no wrong.
> Morning by morning
>> He dispenses His justice,
> and every new day
>> He does not fail."

Tears flooded my eyes and waves of prayer crashed against my heart, spilling out of my mouth and onto the cold tile floor all around me.

"Oh Jesus, bind this crazy, stinking visitor and cast her far from me. Fill me to overflowing with the presence and peace of your Holy Spirit. Restore my joy. Help me be a happy mother for my kids and a contented wife to my husband. Shut out the voices around me. Help me to be whole and wholly in your presence, O God. I know I'm a big, hot mess, but you are bigger and more awesome and more wonderful and I don't have to be amazing and perfect and put together. I just need to be me." I heard a groan from the upstairs bathroom.

Wiping away the tears with the heel of my hand, I read on:

> "The Lord your God is with you,
>> He is mighty to save.

He will take great delight in you;

    He will quiet you with His love,

He will rejoice over you with singing.

"I will gather...I will save...I will bring you in...I will restore."

"Oh my Lord and my God," I whispered, "oh my God.

"Mama?" I looked up to the stairs towards the sound. My nine-year-old daughter stood at the top of the stairs rubbing her eyes. She padded down the steps and ran to me, seemingly unfazed by her mother standing in the middle of the kitchen like a crazy person, screaming passages from the Bible to no one.

"Are you okay, Mama?"

I took her into my arms and kissed the top of her head, breathing in the scent of her. "Yes, baby girl, Mama's more than okay."

# The Wrestler

"For crying out loud, Jim, can't you handle your boys?" Assistant Principal Dick Shannon was beside himself. "I just got off the phone with the boy's mother. I've got to make a decision and fast. You have no idea what kind of position you've put me in."

Coach Jim Mulcahey just shrugged. "How is this *my* fault? Boys do stupid things, Dick. It's who they are."

"Sounds like an excuse to me, Jim. If I tried to pull that kind of crap on my wrestling coach, he'd have thrown me to the mat."

Jim opened his mouth to say more—probably something about the boys being *just* wrestlers or *only* freshman—but Dick shot him a look that said he didn't have a case.

Dick stood and began pacing from his desk, to the wall, and back again. He ran his fingers through his thick hair over and over as if to stimulate brain activity, but he could see no escape.

"How many weeks till state-quals?" Dick asked.

"Three," said Jim.

"Okay, I could suspend the boys for two weeks. They

could be back on the team in time for…"

"Can't," said Jim. "Rules state they've got to compete in *every* remaining meet or they're disqualified for State."

Dick returned to pacing.

Jim went on. "These three boys are the best chance Franklin County High has for a trophy this year. They've never been in trouble before. They show up for practice, keep up their grades, and they're friends with almost everybody. They're good kids, Dick."

Dick stopped pacing and looked at the coach with disbelief. "Good kids don't…"

"It's been eleven years since we even qualified," Jim said.

Dick whirled, lunging at his coach, "I don't give a rat's! What in hell were those little creeps thinking! IDIOTS!" he shouted, slamming the heel of his hand on the desk. Then he fell into his chair and dropped his head in his hands.

This predicament had caught him off balance, and he felt trapped. *Bad for the school, bad for the team, bad for me.*

"If Danny's mother takes legal action and slams the school with harassment charges, a lot more will be at stake than Franklin County's chances for a stupid state title in wrestling, Jim."

Dick had been assistant principal for nine years and was looking toward the head principal's scheduled retirement eighteen months from now. If he maintained a good position, he might have a shot at filling that seat, and, eventually becoming district superintendent.

*I'm so close, so close, and I'm not going to take the fall for anyone—not a coach, not the school, and not a bunch of stupid kids.*

Jim took a deep breath and fiddled with his wristwatch. Thankfully it was not his call to make, and there was no point in locking horns with the assistant principal.

After a few minutes, Jim cleared his throat. "Did Danny come to school today?"

Dick picked up a pen, clicked it in and out nervously, then rolled it between his palms several times before answering, "I don't know. I don't think so."

This time Jim's voice cracked. "H-has his mother come in yet?"

Dick looked the coach square in the face and spoke very slowly. "Tomorrow. So I need to make this decision, before she comes in because…well, for tactical purposes. It's best to deal with these things discreetly and efficiently. I will not be thrown by any, well, by a mother's feelings. Mothers can be, you know…"

"Upset? Emotional? Unreasonable?" Jim offered.

Dick studied the pen in his hands. He knew his position was weak. If the school board put him in a choke hold, there could be legal action and media attention. If he let his feelings onto the floor, he would lose this battle, and likely his career would be over. The humiliation...

Dick set the pen down and leaned back in his chair with his legs straight in front of him. He locked his fingers behind his head, and looked directly at the coach. Jim remained mute and looked back at his colleague, waiting to see if the assistant principal had come to a decision.

"I've got it. I will give the boys morning detention for two weeks. That won't interfere with their schoolwork or with after school practice."

"Morning detention. Good," Jim said, brightening. "That will send a clear message that they can't get away with...doing stupid stuff like this again."

"Have them write an apology, too," Dick said, "to the boy's mother."

"Yeah, yeah, great idea, Dick." Jim was relieved to hear the authority returning to his principal's voice. "I'll help them with the letter, and they can all sign it."

Dick was relieved, too. He stood up and began straightening his shirt and tie. "Okay, Jim. Call the boys in here." His voice was stronger and he cleared his throat again. "This kind of incident won't be happening—*cannot happen*—again, not in my school."

*We're doing the right thing,* Jim thought as he stood up. *This solution is really going to work out the best for everybody.* He lunged for the door and practically ran out of the room.

Ian, Brian, and Eddy were sprawled in chairs by the secretary's desk.

"GET YOUR BUTTS IN HERE NOW!" Jim bellowed. "MOVE, MOVE, MOVE!!"

The boys limped compliantly into the office and closed the door behind them. Jim didn't wait around to hear the bawling out. He had state-quals to prepare for. His head felt lighter as he made his way to the locker rooms.

\*\*\*\*\*\*\*\*\*\*\*\*\*

Dick slung his coat over one arm and strutted down the hall. It was a short move from his former office to the Head Principal's Office, but it had been a long time in coming—ten years, in fact, and now with the retirement luncheon over, everything was official. The position was finally his.

Passing by the trophy case, Dick Shannon noted the

signed football jerseys and team photos peeking out from behind the various trophies the school had accumulated over the years.

Franklin County High School had done well in swimming, track, and basketball. Everyone was especially proud of last year's wrestling team. Having defeated every opponent, they had indeed won the state championship and brought home a wrestling trophy for the first time ever.

Dick flipped on the light in his new office. His secretary had cleared out his old desk; pens, papers and family photos were all jumbled together in a box. He began unpacking and arranging things in his new desk when he came upon a forgotten piece of paper. His breath caught in his throat.

It was a copy of a letter he was supposed to have filed away. He had stuffed it in the back of a drawer almost a year ago and had forgotten about the whole incident. With trembling fingers, he unfolded the letter and began to read the penciled scrawl:

*Dear Mrs. Gresham,*

*We are sorry we held down your son and peed on him yesterday after school. We know this was inappropriate, and we*

*promise we won't do it again. We hope
Danny won't feel bad and he will come
back to school soon. All the kids in his spe
cial needs class miss him a lot.*

> *Sincerely,*
> *Ian Jacobs, Brian Payne, Eddy Mitchell*

Dick fell back in his chair and closed his eyes. Familiar shame drove its head into his chest, like it had so many times before. With his face to the mat, there was nothing to do but admit defeat. He brought his right hand to the top of his big new desk. Like any wrestler who knows he has lost the match, Head Principal Dick Shannon tapped out.

# Tea Party

"And then what did you do, Lady Serena?" Rylie asks me, her eyes twinkling.

"I told the evil fairy, 'Let's put our swords down and make a tea party.'"

Rylie smiles. "A marvelous idea, Lady Serena. Did she do it? Did the evil fairy drink tea with you?"

"She did, and when she put the tea to her lips and drank a little bit, she grabbed at her throat and dropped down dead."

"Poison?" Rylie asks.

"Poison," I say.

"I would have never thought it of you, Lady Serena," Some cookie bits fall from the corner of her mouth.

"Oh, I didn't do it! The Snake King's trusted servant, Dewey the Dwarf, he's the one who poisoned the drink secretly while the Evil Fairy and I were sword fighting."

"What a tale, Lady Serena! You are very brave indeed! And clever, too." Rylie raises her pinky and her eyebrows as she takes a sip from her tea cup. She winks at me over the top of the cup, like she always does, and I try to wink back. Only I'm not very good at it yet, so I just kind of scrunch up my eyes and wiggle my nose instead.

Rylie turns to Mother, "Don't you think so, Kim?"

"Uh-huh," Mother mutters, without looking up.

"Kim?" Rylie asks again.

"What?!" Mother snaps this time and looks up at her sister. Then she gets a bit softer and says, "Oh, yeah, yeah, it was good, honey, really great." She never even looks at me. Her eyes are back on the computer.

Rylie sets her cup down and leans over the table like she's gonna tell me a great secret. "Lady Serena," she whispers really loudly, "I have a tale to tell you as well. It's about an evil stepsister who never gets off her computer even to eat or drink or play. One day she turns into an old tree stump and the Queen's best huntress, Rylie the Great, comes along to chop that old tree down for building a grand bonfire for the king's…"

"Alright, alright," Mother says. "I'm here, I'm doing it. Great tea, Serena, can I have some more?" Mother sounds impatient and looks over at me for the first time. When I had poured some of my best magical raspberry tea with chocolate bits and rainbow sprinkles into Mother's tea cup earlier, she just drank it straight away and turned back to her phone.

Now Mother's face looks like it might crack, but I

pour her some more tea anyway. She doesn't blow on it like Rylie always does, (even though it's just water and it isn't hot one bit.) She makes a loud slurping noise though.

"You sound like a hog drinking tea, Kim," Rylie says. I cover my mouth and laugh.

Mother doesn't lift her pinky and take dainty little sips like me and Rylie do either. And she's completely ignored the little cookies that Rylie brought special for me —*biscuits,* she calls them, like real queens and princesses eat back in England—and she buys them from a special shop and always has some in her purse for when she comes over to visit. While Rylie and I tell tall-tales back and forth to one another, Mother just says "Uh-huh" a lot and I don't know if she's talking to me or talking into that tooth-thingy in her ear.

Rylie's the best for tea parties though. In real life, she's my mother's sister—Aunt Rylie Anne Lipton, like the tea—but I've always called her plain old Rylie and she calls me Lady Serena, even though I'm just Serena. She comes over a lot more these days to help around, since Mother is working longer hours.

Mother is Mother, and I have two brothers, too— Jesse and Frank. (Everyone thinks that's funny that they are named Jesse and Frank. I don't really get it.) They are upstairs most of the time, playing with Legos or something, so I have Rylie all to myself, which is fantastic. Daddy is at his apartment with his new puppy and we go and visit him every other weekend.

"Rylie, some of us have work to do. I can't help it if…" There's a buzzing sound and Mother looks down at the phone in her hand. "Oh, I've got to check that."

"Mother, texting is not for tea parties," I say in my best whiny voice.

"Yeah, Kim, no texting at the tea party," Rylie mimics me. Mother looks up through her eyebrows, annoyed at Rylie, and I giggle again.

"You two fight like Jesse and Frank," I say.

Rylie stands up, and begins stacking our empty plates and cups. "You better believe it, Serena. We could always fight like the best of them." I look at Mother to hear her side of it, but she's too busy with her thumbs on the phone.

"Is our tea party over, Rylie?"

"Well, my lady, I must get about me cooking now. Would you mind terribly joining me in the larder and I shall fetch us some things for a fine supper."

"Wha-a-a-at?" I ask her. Now my face really is scrunched up.

"It means, dear Serena, let's go to the kitchen. I've got

some tuna sandwiches and lemonade to whip up for our lunch."

I giggle at my favorite aunt. "O-kay," I answer back in a silly voice.

She sticks out her elbow and I take a hold of it, hopping down from the bar stool. Rylie walks me, like a real princess, slowly around the bar and into the kitchen-half of the room. We leave mother alone at her side of the counter, but I don't think she even notices we're gone. Her thumbs are still busy.

"So, Lady Serena," Rylie asks as she pulls out a cutting board and a can of tuna, "you never did say: how are the cousins in Norway doing?"

"They're good," I say.

"And how are the kittens next door? Are they enjoying their new washing machine?" she says, kinda loud because she's using the electronic can opener and has to holler a bit over the noise of it.

"The kittens are good," I holler back. "They like to play in the washing machine actually."

"They do?" Rylie turns with surprise. She's squeezing all the juice from the tuna can into the sink, and I know it will make her hands smell fishy. "I didn't think cats enjoyed getting wet," she says.

Rylie is so good at playing along with me. I like it.

"Dan, I know it's *my* weekend." Mother's voice cuts through our play story about the kittens. "I was able to juggle some things around, but I had to give up an important..." She's talking with Daddy. I try to ignore it.

The onion Rylie is cutting up makes her eyes water and she wipes them with the back of her arm. I pick up an apple from the fruit basket at the counter and pick at the sticker till it finally comes off.

"Well, *these* kittens love water actually," I tell Rylie, getting back to my story, "and they take bubble baths in the washing machine right along with the socks and underwear.

Rylie laughs out loud as she waves a spoon of Miracle Whip in the air. "You mean Granny's old socks and panties?"

Mother's stern voice broke in, "What are you telling her, Rylie? Can you keep it down!"

"Yes," I laugh, egging on Mother, "The polka dot panties and the socks with the holes in it." We make the tale taller and taller. It's always so funny to play like this with Rylie. I wish it would never stop.

"The ones she can poke her big toe right through and wave it at us from across the room?"

"Yes, those are the ones! The kittens play hide and seek in those socks."

"I don't care about that, Dan." Mother's voice has gotten so loud. She catches me looking at her and tries to smile at me, but her mouth is still moving to Daddy about something else. Then she lowers her head and her voice. I turn back to Rylie and Granny's socks.

"Well, I heard that Lady Winthrop has holes in her panties, too, and she fills in the torn spots with something so no one will notice. What do you think she uses, Lady Serena?"

"Um...peanut butter, I think."

This cracks her up and Rylie shakes and laughs and tears come into her eyes. I love it when she laughs like that. I wish I could make Mother laugh like that. Nothing is better than a good belly laugh.

"Peanut butter in her panties! That's what's wrong with her then. It all makes sense now!" Rylie puts the top on three sandwiches and then hovers over them with her knife.

"Squares or triangles?" she asks me.

"Triangles!" I say.

"Triangles it is," she says. "And would you get down the potato chips?"

"Sure." I push the kitchen chair across the floor, which makes a terribly delicious racket, and climb up to get the bag of potato chips off the top of the fridge. It seems we're out of the cheesy ones and only have the wavy ones left. No one's favorite.

"Boys!" Rylie hollers, and Jesse and Frank hurtle downstairs with their flying Lego spaceships.

"Hi, Rylie, look at my ship!"

"Mmm, this is very amazing, Jesse. Tell me about all this cool stuff you've got on here."

"Well, these are the heat-seeking machine guns," my little brother says, pointing at some red-colored blocks, "and these are where the gazillion bullets are stored for emergencies," he says again, pointing at some gray-colored blocks.

"And these are my…"

"Let me have a chance," Frank butts in. "I made a ship, too." He points out all the guns and cannons and flaming nun chucks and other boy stuff that's on his ship, and Rylie seems real interested.

"Here's a bunch more stuff. There's a mace, ninja stars, double-bladed swords, a sickle, an ax and a double-bladed ax, and bombs and grenade-throwers and rocket-launchers."

"Sounds terribly exciting," Rylie says, examining each thing as my big brother points it out.

Mother sighs from behind her computer screen, and Frank gets quiet all of a sudden.

Rylie passes his Lego ship back and ruffles his hair. "Go wash your hands, boys, and we'll have lunch." Both my brothers look like a balloon that just had all the air taken out at once.

"We have chips, too!" I say, even if they're just the wavy ones.

The boys sound like elephants going up the stairs to the bathroom. Next thing you know, they're fussing and jabbering and the water is running upstairs, so I know they're feeling better again.

Rylie washes two apples and starts slicing them up.

"So, Lady Serena, you never did tell me what happened after your tea party with the evil fairy."

Mother is still talking to Daddy. "I'm going to the gym during lunch, and my nails are at four, so I'll be over with the kids after that." I'm still ignoring her.

"The evil fairy was poisoned, so I hopped on a hot air balloon and flew back to the castle."

Mother shouts, "Get off yourself, Dan!"

"I picked flowers for the royal banquet and passed them out to all the fairy princesses who came to the party."

Rylie says, "That was nice of you."

Mother says, "This is my life, too. Don't I have a right to be happy?"

"Then I met a dragon who seemed real nice at first, but then…" my voice trails off.

"Then what?" Rylie asks.

"Then I suppose after all these years of sacrifice, I'm supposed to just lay down and…" Mother is shouting.

"Then I just laid down," I say. "Inside the dragon's cave…"

"I think I need a break, Dan."

"And the dragon leans over me with his big teeth and his drooling, bad breath…"

"Maybe you should have them for a while."

"And I can see the stars twinkling out of the mouth of the cave…"

"Boys, come down and eat!" Rylie calls.

"Fine." Mother says quietly. "I'll make final arrangements with the lawyers and get back to you."

"And I close my eyes…"

"Death to bad guys and pirates!" Frank shouts as he thunders down the stairs with Jesse behind him.

"Death to bad guys!" Jesse echoes.

"Bye." Mother says

"And I die there in the cave…"

"Be careful with your cups, boys," says Rylie.

"…with the dragon there crying over my dead body…"

Mother stands up to leave. "I'll see you later, Rylie. I've got to get back to work. Give Mother a kiss, boys."

"Yeah, okay. Bye, Mom," Frank says, distracted by the chips on his plate.

Mother leans over me and kisses the top of my forehead. "Thanks for the tea party, honey. I'll see you later."

"Uh-huh," I say. I look down at my triangle tuna. The chips look even wavier through my tears. My hand shakes as I try to pick up my cup of lemonade. I just peer into the cup with waves of pink inside.

"…and no one knows whatever happened to me. The end."

Rylie's hand is on my back and her face comes close to mine. I can see her sad smile reflected in my lemonade. "It'll be okay, honey. Your mother loves you, your daddy loves you, and I love you.

"I know," I say quietly.

"And don't forget, Lady Serena, you are a very brave young lady. If you can survive the evil fairy, you can survive anything."

"I love you, too, Rylie." My words sound kinda choked up inside, and my throat feels tight.

She ruffles my hair. I take a bite of my tuna triangle. I feel a little better, but I don't think Rylie's tears are from the onions this time.

# Transfiguration

Dedicated to Imogene Herdman, who changed me

It's so muggy and stuffy in the choir loft I can scarcely breathe up in here. They must have turned the thermostat up to eighty for all the old people in the congregation. It doesn't help that Natty Washburn is behind me every Sunday with his nasty cigarette breath, breathing down my neck. I expect he's been smoking since he was three. I heard his own Pop got him started on it, and he's been at it ever since.

If only lung cancer didn't take so long.

I got in trouble with Mama last week when Natty stood next to me, snickering during communion. I don't know why Natty thinks he's in any right mind—or heart either—to be taking communion. I later explained to Mama that I wasn't the one who was laughing, but it's guilt by association I guess.

"We are respectful, Michaela," Mama said this morning while pulling up her pantyhose. "Church is for honoring God together as a family." Mama's serious voice always accompanies a glare in my direction to further press her *I hope you're understanding me, young lady* message into my head. Maybe she thinks if her words settle down deep into my brain, she won't have to repeat herself so much. I doubt that works on my brother. I closed my eyes and imagined myself rolling my eyes at Mama. There's no way I'd have really done it.

"We dress up in our best. We listen to God's Word. And we don't giggle during communion!"

It was so hard to reason with her while she was doing the panty hose dance right in front of me. I don't need to tell you my explanations fell on deaf ears. She said I'd better not even flinch at a spider on the back of my pew today, or I'd be doing my little brother's chores for a week.

"Singing in the children's choir, in front of God and everybody," she hollered back over her shoulder as she walked around locking up the house, isn't the time to be tickled by the Spirit of God." She stopped at the door to glower at me through what was left of her eyebrows—she had practically plucked them all out before I was even born. Then we both put on a happy face and walked to church in the snow.

Today's sermon must be about sin because all the hymns we're singing seem to be about sin. The whole congregation joins the choir in singing:

*"I was sinking deep in sin..."*

Then Natty and some other boys behind me go, "Wheeee!"

I will *not* look at him. I will *not* look at him. I will *not* look at...ah, there goes Mama frowning at me.

When we get to the chorus, we all sing:

*"Love lifted me..."*

Then the boys behind me echo, "Let me down, let me down!"

*"Love lifted me."* "Let me down!"

Natty Washburn! What is he thinking?! Somebody's gonna hear him, and then we're all gonna get it. I can't say what I'm thinking but I'm thinking it.

I can't smack him on the back of the head either, but I'm thinking about doing that, too. He's already got one goose egg under his cowlick. No one's dared ask him what happened, and he doesn't care enough to tell any of us about it either. Probably his Pop gave it to him. I'd like to give him another one to match.

I sing the rest of the song from memory, determined not to look behind me or at Mama neither. It's best to focus on something that won't get me into trouble.

The wooden pews are dotted with all kinds of cushions for the old people. On the front row, Mr. Alfred uses a blue back cushion that's fat and pudgy, but his wife,

Miss Charlene, doesn't use any because she's plump enough already. Mr. Alfred uses a wooden cane, too, dark and carved to look like some kind of animal head, only he's worn it so smooth by his hand, I can't tell what kind of animal it was supposed to be anymore. If I had a cane like that, I'd chase Natty out of church. He doesn't belong here. He's got no respect.

Behind them sit two old maids, Miss Flossie and Miss Myrtle. Mama says it isn't nice to say that they're old maids, but it's the truth. They're both tall and skinny, and their flowery dresses hang on them like flour sacks.

Both of them have curly hair that's dyed funny. Miss Flossie's looks kind of blue-black and Miss Myrtle's, well, I can't put my finger on it, but that shade of reddish-brown just doesn't look natural. They're sweet old maids though, not crabby like you'd expect for never having found husbands and all.

Once they had me over for a sleepover at their house when I was little. I don't remember whose idea that was, but I think it was more for them than for me. Since they never married nor had any kids of their own, I guess it was kind of special to have one over for a while.

They fixed hominy with supper and flapjacks at breakfast. We watched an old TV show about Mel's Diner, and I slept under a white lacey bed cover and pink sheets with Miss Myrtle. She wore some kind of old-timey night cap like I'd seen in *The Night Before Christmas* book. I stayed awake most of the night though, trying not to listen to her snoring and trying not to look at her teeth perched on the night stand, smiling at me in the moonlight.

Their older brother, Mr. Jarvis, sits on the pew next to them. He and his wife part ways every Sunday morning cause she's a Methodist and he's a Baptist. Mama's never said anything about that, but I bet she's got a strong opinion on it.

Mr. Jarvis owns the general store at the end of our road, and it's just like those old timey shows on TV. There's a big old scale on the porch for weighing cows or something. Men are leaning back in cane-bottom chairs, chewing tobacco and spitting in a coffee can. Mama don't like me going there much, but it's on my way home from school, and besides that, I ain't planning to get caught.

They still sell penny candy at his store. Miss Elspeth—that's Mr. Jarvis's wife, the Methodist—she says to pick one, and I give her my handful of pennies. I always pick bubble gum, but they're so old, I about near break my teeth off.

"Do we have any birthdays this week?" the music

minister booms cheerfully. Every Sunday Brother Dale gets up, places his hands on the sides of the pulpit with his two wrinkly elbows sticking out like chicken wings, and asks about the birthdays and anniversaries.

Natty Washburn shoves me as he makes his way down to the organ. Oh brother.

"Well, Natty Washburn," says Brother Dale, "how old are you, young man?"

"Thirteen, sir." I'm surprised he had enough manners to say *sir*.

"Well, that's fine, Mr. Washburn, and it is a privilege to honor you in song this morning."

*"Happy Birthday to you…"*

A little white church bank is perched on the back of the organ. The tiny door is painted blue and the little plastic windows are made to look like stained-glass. While we all sing, the birthday person is supposed to stick in a couple dollars for the Hope Town Orphan's Home. The Women's Ministry uses it to buy dolls and catcher's mitts at Christmas and fill up Easter baskets in the spring.

Natty's cheeks are red. I bet it's because he doesn't have any money to put in the bank. I wouldn't put it past him to lean over, fake like he's putting money inside, and try to pull some out instead.

The Washburns live in a trailer that's half falling down and half put back together again with scrap wood and sheet metal. It looks more like a chicken coop than a house fit to live in. Mrs. Washburn run off, they say, because she's never been around for as long as I can remember. Mama says Mr. Washburn's a drunk and collects checks from the government instead of working. Natty's got an older brother who's off with a wife and a couple kids. Natty's the only one anybody ever sees much of. Sometimes at church, sometimes at school, everyday riding his bike up and down the dirt roads around here.

He doesn't shove me when he comes back up to the choir loft and sits down. The sneer isn't on his face no more.

"Practices for our annual Easter Cantata will start tonight…"

I'm too excited to listen to the rest of Brother Dale's announcements. Every year our church puts on a play to beat all plays, and everyone in town comes to watch. The Methodists have one man with a bushy black beard, and he looks just like Jesus, so we borrow him every year to be in our show. The deacons play the apostles and the Women's Ministry dress up everybody else to be the townspeople. Most of the kids pass out programs, seat people in the pews when they come in, or sing with the choir. The pastor's son even brings in a real donkey from some old lady who doesn't even come to our church. They probably have to pay her a little money every time we use it.

Every year two older kids are chosen to dress up in costume and run up and down the aisles saying, "Jesus is coming, Jesus is coming." Now that I'm twelve, I'm sure I'll be the girl that's picked. The boy will probably be the preacher's son. He's so tall and well-behaved.

Natty starts breathing on me and sniggering again to Joey, so I only catch snatches of the pastor's praying over the offering.

"Our Heavenly Father…the shut-ins that couldn't be with us this morning…speak to us through your Word, Lord God, and…"

The preacher's voice is all deep and respectful when he's in the pulpit. I don't think God cares much for the way some folks talk to him out in the parking lot, like he's just regular folks, all syrupy and friendly. Mama says it isn't fitting to talk to a man of God that way, even if Jesus did come down as a man himself.

My toes, which long to wiggle through the dew-covered grass of a summer morning, feel hot inside my white tights and winter boots. Easter's just a few weeks away but nobody's told winter anything about it. The snow has dripped off the bottoms of my shoes and left a puddle on the floor at my feet.

Since Mama hurried me this morning, my hair was still damp when I gathered it up into a ponytail and left for church. It feels wretched now. We're supposed to be praying, but I can't help picking at it and digging at it with my fingers. I look over and see Mama's got her stern face on. I close my eyes quick so I won't see her looking at me, in case I get to fidgeting again.

I imagine my hair glossy and smooth, shining in the spotlight at the Easter Cantata. When I'm chosen to...

"...we ask it in the name of your son, Jesus, and all God's people said..."

This is when the congregation usually says, "Amen," but this time all I hear is a resounding, *buuurrrp* from behind my right ear.

No one else lets on that they heard but, boy, am I ready to knock that guy's block off.

"Come, come, children," the preacher's wife says. "It's time for our Bible story." All us big kids head down out of the choir loft and the littler ones get pushed forward by their parents as they head up the aisles and sit around on the floor by the altar steps. I sit as far away from Natty Washburn as I can.

Miss Joy Lee uncovers the flannel board to reveal a

paper Jesus, paper Peter and papers James and John standing around on a paper mountain top. Two paper old guys are there, too. All the old guys in the Bible look the same on a flannel board: Abraham, Noah, Moses — at least I can't tell them apart. I think Miss Joy Lee just recycles the same paper old guys for the different stories.

"Boys and girls, since it's getting closer to Easter time, today's story is called *The Transfiguration*. She reaches back like Vanna White to smooth the paper Peter, who is starting to bow his head in prayer and asks, "Do any of you boys and girls know this story?"

Some *know-it-all* second-grader in glasses raises his hand. When Miss Joy Lee looks like she might call on him, he quickly ducks his head down and giggles. The rest of us keep our hands down so Miss Joy Lee will just get on with it.

I barely catch any of the story—something about Jesus being transfigured on top of a mountain. Miss Joy Lee puts some golden streaks behind Jesus' head and body. He's supposed to look all *glowy* and everything, I don't really get it.

I think my outfit for the cantata should be green with brown and white stripes, not too flashy, real authentic.

The preacher's wife winds up the story just as the little kids start getting squirrely. "Boys and girls, this year's head boy and girl to perform in the Easter Cantata will be Michaela Alcorn…"

It's me! It's me!

"And Nathaniel Washburn."

Oh no! Kill me now.

\*\*\*\*\*\*\*\*\*\*\*\*\*

It's the night of the performance, and I did get to dress up in the striped gown I'd been hoping for. While Mama waited in her usual pew, wearing her best *go-to-meeting* hat, I snuck downstairs to the women's bathroom and combed my hair two hundred times so it would glisten in the spotlight.

Natty looked like a street urchin when he did his part, running up and down between the pews in his bare feet with his dirty brown hair sticking up all over, announcing the arrival of the Messiah. I kept expecting him to try something foolish to mess up the performance. It would be just like him to use cat calls when Jesus rode in on the donkey, whoops and whistles when he ran the merchants out of the temple with whips, and burps during the Last Supper with the disciples.

The whole sanctuary is dark except for the stage. But Brother Dale has all us kids sitting in the last pew in case the boys get to fooling around and disturbing folks.

Up on the stage the soldiers are prodding Jesus along with their spears into the spotlight. He's nearly naked and dragging his heavy cross on one shoulder behind him. The Women's Ministry have concocted some kind of goo and smeared it all over his chest and arms. When I got up close to him during dress rehearsal, I could smell a tar smell, along with all the aftershave and man-sweat. From a distance, though, that fake blood looks pretty realistic and kind of frightening.

The soldiers force Jesus behind the baptistery curtain where they plan to *crucify* him. A plank has been laid across the pool for standing on and the pastor's son put dry ice all around so Jesus' feet are hidden in the white smoke.

When the soldiers pretend to hammer the nails into his hands, Jesus cries out, and Natty gets real stiff next to me. I peek over at him since he can't see me in the dark and wait for my eyes to get used to it.

Natty's staring straight ahead! Like he can't take his eyes off Jesus! His cheeks are glistening, and a big tear falls down Natty's cheek.

From the stage, I hear Jesus groan, "It is finished," and I know this is the part where he slumps down dead on the cross, but I miss the whole thing because I can't stop staring at Natty. He's sniffling and wiping his face with the sleeve of his costume, just like you'd expect him to do. But even then, Natty still looks a little...*glowy.*

The spotlight goes out, and the preacher's wife starts playing the piano real soft in the corner. The whole congregation is supposed to sit in the dark and meditate on their sins and how they need to accept Jesus, since he died and all. This is the part where Jesus sneaks away to get cleaned up for the big resurrection scene that everyone knows is coming.

I can't think about that now. I can't think about anything but Natty. I can't believe Natty Washburn is all shook up about this. What does he know about Jesus and God and Easter and everything?

Natty's nothing but gross and dirty and rude. Coming to church every Sunday has never had any effect on him during the rest of the week. He's still the one who's always pulling pranks and cheating on tests.

Why he, he…why I, I could never, I would never show my face again if I had done all the sinning he's done. In the dark I give Natty my Mama's best look of disapproval.

Everybody and their cousin is here tonight—blowing their noses, crying, and sniffling. I don't know why *I'm* not crying. I love God and Jesus. Anybody can tell whose side *I'm* on, plain as day.

I can't stand it.

I hunch over where no one can see me and quietly spit into my hands. I pat that spit around good and thick over my eyes and cheeks so when the light come on, I'll be the one who's glistening and glowy.

# Comfort Zone

Jared closed his eyes. He couldn't think. The crying had been insistent for what seemed like hours. Now it was right up next to his ear, under his chin and inconsolable. He tried a few tentative jiggles as he had seen his wife do. Tina flopped face down on top of the bed, beside herself with fatigue. He began to sway and hum.

"Hm, hm, hmmm. Hm, hm, hmmm. Hm, hm, hm, hm, hmmmmm." The combined swaying, jiggling, and humming was kind of tricky, but as he looked to his wife for confirmation he could see in the glow of the side-table lamp that she was conked out. He continued to sway and hum as he backed out of the room and headed toward the den, simulating his wife's swinging-hips by taking long steps from side to side.

The wailing infant in his arms began hiccupping between sobs. Jared was inclined to hum louder, but he thought better of it and switched to singing the tune instead.

"Jingle bells, jingle bells…" Jared's body flowed back and forth through the dark house like an apparition.

"Jingle all the way." It was frustrating that he couldn't think of a different song, but this one was the only one that came to mind, even if it was the middle of March.

He continued to jiggle as he felt along the wall till he reached the doorway of his man-cave. Without thinking, he flipped on the light, and his baby girl flinched.

"Oh, oh, sorry baby," he whispered. In a matter of half-seconds, Jared mapped out where the recliner was over by the window and located the crocheted afghan on the back of the loveseat. Then he snatched off the light and moved toward the recliner, leaning over to scoop up the afghan along the way.

The baby on his arm had grown still and quiet the moment he turned the light off, but Jared kept up his soft singing and jiggling as he sashayed down into the chair, pulled back the lever to raise the foot rest, and struggled to arrange the afghan around the little one curled up on his shoulder. His own legs and feet were left exposed, and a shiver ran through him. He had not noticed until now how chilly the house had become.

His jiggling slowed to a stop. His singing faded to a whisper. His ears were taut with anticipation, listening and waiting to see if his efforts had paid off. The infant settled herself into the crook of Jared's neck and seemed to curl up in an even tighter ball. He inhaled the new baby smell of her—no words could describe its sweetness—like heaven itself lay inches from his face.

The little body cradled in his big hands was growing limper as her hiccupping and sobbing subsided. Jared could feel the warmth of her on his neck. Her curly brown hair was damp from exertion. Despite his own fatigue and cold feet, there was no place in the world he'd rather be.

"Ch, ch, ch," he whispered into the air, closing his eyes. "Daddy's here, Gracie, Daddy's here."

*************

"See me dance, Daddy. Do you like my style?"

Jared looked up from his recliner where he'd been watching a soccer game on his laptop. "Wow. *Style*? How do you know a word like *style*?"

Four-year-old Gracie was in a pink ballerina dress, a reindeer ski cap, and cowboy boots. Her *style,* as she called it, charmed him to his toes.

"Da-ddy," she said, dropping her shoulders and swinging her arms down around her knees, "I watch cartoons. On TV."

Jared stifled his grin. "Oh, really, how could I not have known?"

Gracie burst out laughing, "You're so funny, Daddy."

"Oh, you think so?!" With care, Jared set the laptop on the side table and slung the foot rest down. "You think I'm funny? You think I'm funny?" He flung his arms out and scooped the preschooler up in his arms. She squealed as he slung her over his shoulder and pranced around the room. She flopped with wild laughter.

Tossing her onto the sofa, he began to crawl his fingers all over her body, gently pinching her tummy and cheeks and bottom. Her abandoned giggling morphed into a fit of hiccups.

"Jared," scolded Tina, from the doorway, "she won't be able to stop, and it's almost bedtime."

With a devilish gleam, Jared said, "If I can't tickle her, then I'll have to EAT HER UP!"

A splendid cacophony ensued as Tina looked on—Gracie's hysterical whooping between her hiccups and Jared's growling over her.

Breathless, Jared sat back on the couch. Father and daughter stared at each other, wheezing and thoroughly pleased with one another.

"Do it again, Daddy," Gracie hiccupped.

"Are you kidding?" Jared panted. "Are you kidding?" he said again, accompanied by one final tickle to the tummy. "You wore Daddy out, Grace. I'm pooped."

"You're pooped," the preschooler guffawed. "I'm

telling Mommy you pooped." Ski cap missing and hair awry, she headed toward the kitchen. Jared used the heels of both hands to wipe the tears that had formed in his eyes from laughing so hard. He took a deep breath and let it out in a heavy rush of satisfaction.

*Clip-clop, clip-clop* went Gracie's too-big boots. Then she stopped unexpectedly, turned back and *clip-clopped* back to Jared's side again.

"Did you forget something, pumpkin?"

"I forgot to kiss you, Daddy." She leaned over the arm rest and, standing up on tiptoe in her boots, her tiny, wet lips met the corner of his mouth and melted his heart clean away.

\*\*\*\*\*\*\*\*\*\*\*\*\*

"Gross, Dad, how can you eat that stuff?"

"Eggs and toast? How can I eat eggs and toast?"

"Poached eggs are so…" She shuddered. "Nasty."

"Okay, wise guy, and what are you eating for breakfast? Cereal? Cardboard flakes with red food coloring and sugar? Give me a break."

Gracie walked by with the cereal box and shoved her father in the shoulder.

Jared looked up in surprise, "You wanna piece of me?

You wanna step outside and see who is who in this relationship? Huh? Huh?"

The twelve-year-old snorted as she pulled back the chair across from him. Jared made a funny face in his daughter's direction.

Tina spoke up from the rim of her coffee cup by the sink. "Okay, you two, I see where this is headed and there's no time for it this morning. We've got to go, so hurry up and eat."

Jared continued to look at his daughter and gave a slow wink.

"I mean it," Tina snarled, but she was laughing as she spoke.

"So, Grace," Jared asked, biting into his buttered toast, "what's on the agenda for today?"

"A vocab test in Millman's class. Uh, some algebra-something, I can't remember. And I have to run the mile in gym."

"Ooh, exciting stuff. I always did look good in gym shorts. With my bulging muscles and my manly, hairy legs in knee socks."

"Ew," Gracie said.

"You mean chicken legs in knee socks, don't you?" Tina said as she rinsed out the coffee pot and placed it upside down in the dish rack.

"I'll have you know," Jared began, rising with his empty plate in hand.

Gracie groaned, "Not the *'I was the fastest sprinter in my class and I won the gold for Morrison Junior High School and made the girls swoon over my awesome speed and dexterity'* story again."

"Oh, have you heard that story before?" Jared said. "Am I boring you with my tales of my amazingness and athletic prowess?" He moved in closer behind Grace's chair. "Me thinks thou dost protest too much, fair damsel."

She stood up with her empty cereal bowl in hand and looked at her dad through hooded brows, "What-ever," she said in her best bratty teenage voice.

"Come on, you two."

"You're just jealous," Jared said, strutting by his daughter with his nose in the air.

Grace tiptoed behind him and put a hand on Jared's shoulder, "Oh, Daddy, you know I was just…" then she dashed by, making a break for the front door. Snatching up her backpack and jacket, she yelled back, "I'll show you who's fastest. Shotgun!"

"What-ever!" Jared called after her as he grabbed his own cell phone, set of keys and computer bag from the couch. "Do you hear me? What-ever!"

✱✱✱✱✱✱✱✱✱✱✱✱✱

Jared could just make out the small glowing numbers across the room: *10:27*. Three minutes, three minutes. She was probably outside in his car having a long good-bye. He grimaced and squeezed his eyes shut, not wanting to think about it.

Sixteen was too young to be out with boys really. Who came up with this nonsense that girls should be allowed to go out with boys when they are sixteen? And who came up with the brilliant idea to let these idiot, speed-happy boys drive fast cars when they were still so young and stupid and out till all hours with his daughter?

Tina had said repeatedly that it was a compromise: no boyfriends till she was sixteen and she had to be home by 10:30.

"Where's the compromise?" Gracie wanted to know, protesting that most of her friends had been dating since junior high and their curfews were all midnight or one o'clock.

"If Daddy had his way, it would be no boyfriends till your thirty and a curfew of eight o'clock. Cut us some slack, Grace. No good comes from being out with high school boys past ten o'clock. Trust me."

Gracie's hair, which she painstakingly straightened every morning before school, hung over one eye, partly hiding the hormone-driven emotions which lay bare on her face.

When had his little girl gotten so grown up in her skinny jeans and form-fitting tee shirts? When had she gotten so headstrong and exasperating?

Whenever the two women had to duke it out, Jared pretended to be part of the wallpaper over by the coffee-maker or kept himself tucked away in his man-cave with the door only partway open.

Now it was 10:31 and he heard a car door slam. *Ahhh.* He relaxed. He listened for the expected sounds—the keys jangling in the lock, the squeak of the front door, and his daughter's feet on the carpeted stairs that led to her room. All the usual sounds came and went. He could go back to sleep, thankful that another Saturday night was over.

Tina slept next to him, her breathing soft and deep. Jared flipped his pillow and sank down into the coolness, readying himself to fall back to sleep, too.

Then he heard it through the vent in his ceiling— muffled sobbing from upstairs.

*What has happened?!*

Deciding not to wake his wife and ignoring the robe and slippers nearby, Jared crossed his arms against the chill of the house and headed upstairs in his tee shirt and flannel pants. Gracie's door was open a crack, and her light was off. He could just make out her silhouette in the dark, like a lump on the bed, racked with quiet sobs.

His voice caught in his throat as he called to her from the door. "Grace, Gracie? Honey, are you okay?"

The crying stopped and she rolled over to look toward the doorway. "Daddy?"

Without waiting for permission, Jared rushed to the bedside and sat down. His eyes began adjusting to the darkness. He hadn't been in Gracie's room in such a long time. The pink wallpaper of a ballerina-loving little girl had long been covered up by posters of boys and bands and abstract art. Even though she acted tough and grown up so much of the time, her room was still littered with stuffed bears. Heart-shaped pillows were scattered on the foot of her bed.

"What happened, Grace?" His voice was soft at first and then, contemplating the possibilities, it rose to a snarl as he jumped back to his feet, "Did he touch you? Did he hurt you? Gracie, did he…?"

Gracie started crying again. Jared was beside himself with anger and helplessness. He looked around and spotted the Strawberry Shortcake lampshade in the moonlight. He fumbled up under it and flipped the switch. Both of them squinted against the light for a few seconds.

Then he was reaching out for her, drawing her shoulders away from the pillow and peering into her tear-streaked face.

Her words tumbled out in a rush, "I thought," she sniffled and wiped her nose with the back of her hand, "I was ready, Daddy, please don't be disappointed in me. I'm sorry."

Jared stiffened. He would make plans to kill the boy later. Sitting back, he said nothing. He knew his face looked stony and he made an effort to soften it.

"I didn't do it, Daddy, I promise, but we started to. I let...I let him touch me...a little bit. And then I knew I wasn't ready. I started crying, and I made him drive me home. I'm so sorry, Daddy, I've ruined everything." She hung her head and sobbed.

Jared hung his head, too. He was grieved and also relieved. His little girl was still his little girl. For that, he was thankful. With tenderness, he reached out for her convulsing shoulders and pulled her in for a tight hug. With his arms clutching her huddled body like a life preserver, he laid his cheek against the top of her head, and rocked back.

"Ch, ch, ch, ch, Daddy's here. Daddy's here."

*Oh, baby,* he thought, *oh my little girl, how I have wanted to protect you from this. Protect you from making these grown-up decisions with boys who don't care about anything but that one thing. I'm so sorry, honey. I'm so sorry.*

After several long minutes, her breathing calmed. She stopped crying.

"Gracie," he said, his voice cracking with emotion, "look at me." He waited. She wiped her nose and face on the bottom of her sweater before looking into her daddy's tear-rimmed eyes.

"I am so sorry this happened, baby." When she cried, she looked like the little girl he knew so well. She couldn't be sixteen already. It didn't seem possible.

"I love you, Gracie. I wish I could make it better." He looked down at the fuzzy bedspread.

"I'm sorry I fought with you and Mom about dating and stuff. I was so stupid. I'm sorry I've been such a, you know, I've been so rude to you and Mom lately."

"Sweetheart," he said with renewed strength in his voice, pulling her back into his arms, "You're going to get through this. You're growing up into a fine woman. It'll come soon enough."

As he spoke, he stroked her hair, its fine brown strands falling over his wide fingers as he clung to her with fierceness and tenderness. "I'm proud of you, Gracie. I hope you know that."

She mumbled into his chest, "I'm not proud of me, Daddy. I've made such a mess of my life."

He pulled back to look at her. "What are you talking about—a mess of your life? Your life's just starting. We all make mistakes. Sometimes we hurt ourselves, sometimes others. Some mistakes take a long time to get over, but we all do it. His tone changed, "I know it's hard to believe, but even I have done some stupid stuff." She giggled.

"It's all going to work out, pumpkin. You've got a lot of living left to do; and there are other boys—better boys—who will wait for you and move at your pace. A slow pace would be good," he teased. "A married pace would be better. It never hurts to wait for those important things, but it can definitely hurt *not* to."

"I want to do things right, Dad. I want you and Mom to be proud of me."

"Oh, baby, I am so proud of you." Jared cupped her chin in his hand. "You're smart, you're funny, you're caring, you're hard-working. You're beautiful."

"Really, Daddy?"

He winked and patted the top of her head. "I think I should go get Mom."

"Okay," she said. He could see she was still upset, but her face seemed more peaceful now. He stood up and walked toward the door, then stopped.

"I almost forgot." He walked back toward the bed, leaned down, and pointed to his cheek. Gracie grabbed his head in her hands and kissed his cheek near the corner of his mouth.

"Thank you, Daddy," she whispered.

"Hey kid, I like your style."

# The Other Woman

Stuart stepped onto his front porch, easing the screen door closed behind him. The sky, startling in its blackness, beckoned him to join her. He took the three steps down from the porch and winced at the ache in his lower back. Taking the night sky up on her invitation, Stuart shoved his hands in his pockets and headed out onto the gravel road.

Amy was still inside. He tried not to think of her, sitting at the computer, stroking keys like her life depended on it. Maybe it did. He had been sober for two years but the damage had been done between them over their decades together before. Stuart squeezed the muscles in his face to stop the tears that trembled in his eyes.

"Can you grab something from the fridge for your dinner?" she had said. "I'm so busy." He had headed toward the kitchen but no longer felt hungry. Innocuous words, really, but all too significant—all too telling of what their marriage had become, what his life had become. He had skipped dinner and headed outside.

If Stuart had known twenty-nine years ago what love and romance would become, what he would become, he might have struck out on the road with his guitar like he had planned and never looked back. With the wide sky outside and music inside, there would have been no wife to squeeze him in between business trips, or keep him dangling at arm's length. No wound in his heart to continually tend with the passing seasons.

Stuart's pace quickened in the chill night. By the time the first tear slid down his cheek, he had journeyed far enough down the gravel road he was out of reach of the porch light. Through his tears he could see stars piercing the blackness. Loose rock crunched pleasantly beneath his heavy footfalls as he pressed on. He swallowed hard against the familiar knot in his throat.

That guitar he had played in college had loved being held. His uncle had given it to him when he was ten years old and only half its size. He could hardly reach his fingers around the neck to press the strings. But Stuart grew up, and he grew in love with everything about that sweet guitar.

Taylor was her name, and her neck was slender beneath his fingers. She trembled whenever he stroked her, and he could make her sing with the slightest touch.

Through those early years, his fingertips became hard while his heart remained tender. Even when he would play almost rough in his passion, she would sing all the louder in his grasp.

Then he met Amy and fell in love with her. During the early months of their courtship, Stuart played his guitar and wooed Amy with love songs, composing a new one almost every day. She cooed and fawned over his musical dreams at first, but as the wedding date drew nearer, his drinking increased and so did their fights. Amy turned hard toward Taylor and, more often than not, directed her to stay in a corner so Stuart could "gain respectable employment and become a responsible man."

Stuart snuck in dates when he could but felt torn and vowed to become more the man Amy believed he could be.

Amy and Stuart married, bought a house, and settled into a routine. Stuart woke up cheerful, worked hard all day, and came home eager to talk with his wife about his day.

Amy worked late, watched TV till late, and hurried out of the house early five mornings a week. This had been her habit after the first year. On Saturdays she would have *me* time—launching herself into her car and heading to a friend's house with scrapbooking crates in hand. Stuart wouldn't see her all day, catching only a glimpse of her white night gown as it shimmered over her body right before bed.

Stuart envied the car, the crates, the friend, even the nightgown. They got to spend time with her, hear her stories, make her laugh, and touch her soft, white skin. He got the condensed version of her day on Sunday morning as they headed to church.

"How's Marcy?"

"Great."

"Did you get a lot done yesterday?"

"Four pages maybe."

"Good, good. What year are you up to now?"

"I don't know, a couple of summers ago I think."

"Nice…is that when we went on our Missouri trip?"

"Yeah, Missouri."

*"How was your day, Stuart?"* he mused to himself. *"Did you have a nice Saturday? Did you miss me while I was gone? Do you miss me all the times that I'm gone? Do you miss me now? Who needs church this morning? Why don't you hang a left and we'll go catch a movie? No? We could go for a walk in the park instead? Oh, Stuart, I would love to hold your hand and tell you stories and hear you laugh. I would love to have you lay with me in the grass and have you touch me like, like…I would love to…I would love you."*

"I would love to get to church on time, Stuart. Would you drive a bit faster please?"

Stuart wondered now as he plodded on down the gravel road if Amy missed him, if she even knew he was gone. Or even cared. They both knew he could go back to the bottle any time.

The gravel ended abruptly under Stuart's feet and pavement formed a straight black line in front of him. He didn't have his watch on but it seemed like he'd been gone for nearly an hour, maybe longer. Now he was at the highway. He could keep walking. The path looked a lot smoother up ahead. He could stay out another few minutes.

Maybe longer. Maybe forever.

Without a sound, Stuart turned his feet around and headed back to the house. The stars seemed to be all behind him now. The gravel was sharp and dug into the bottoms of his shoes. The ache in his back returned. He pulled his stiff hands out of his pockets and pressed his thumbs hard on either side of his spine.

The journey back seemed shorter, and Stuart was sorry for it. He stepped up onto the porch, gingerly opened the screen door, and walked through the dark kitchen toward the flickering light of the bedroom.

"Hi, sweetheart," he said from the doorway, "can I get you anything?"

"I'm fine," Amy said without looking away from the

TV. He stood there, studying her. She was stretched out on the bed, her white night gown clung to her curves and shimmered in the flickering light. The ache in his back moved into his chest. His mouth grew moist and the familiar knot in his throat returned.

Amy's neck was slender. Her breasts were soft mounds under the material. Her waist, hips, and thighs—all the curves were still there, but her arms lay limp. She didn't reach out to him like the sky had done. There was no beckoning here, no invitation to join her.

"Coming to bed?" she asked, her eyes never leaving the television screen.

He thought about it. "Not yet," he said. "Sleep well, Amy."

"Uh-huh," she said.

Stuart turned away from his wife and headed to the basement. There was a guest room down there where someone waited for him. A slender neck that longed to be held, a body that waited to be stroked, a song that beckoned to be sung, and Stuart thought he couldn't wait another minute to make her tremble.

# Saturday

Saturday was born early on a muggy July morning with a chocolate milk moustache. She was hot and barefoot and tickled the tops of the trees with her cool laughter as she descended upon the earth.

When Saturday was four, wearing pigtails and last year's dress, she ate pancakes for breakfast with thick pats of butter and lots of syrup. If there were friends to play with, she went to the park to shimmy down the slide, climb on the monkey bars, or have a picnic lunch. Other times, she stayed home alone, taking a slow spin on the tire swing under her cottonwood tree. She spun and spun until she fell over from joy and dizziness, but it was always worth it.

Sometimes she just sat quietly on the tire and dragged her toe through the dirt.

Six-year-old Saturday never had to be anywhere fast. She spent all her time outside, lining up rocks on the shadow of a flag pole, kicking stones or kicking cans. Sometimes she studied ants marching down the sidewalk or dust floating by in a ray of sunlight. Every afternoon, she beat Grandpa at Checkers and Go Fish. Then she blew bubbles in the backyard with her companions, Chase and Giggle.

Eight-year old Saturday often had scraped knees and dirty hands. Hot afternoons meant popsicle-juice was running down her elbows. She wrestled in the grass with the dog, trying not to get her face licked but not really caring if she did. On rainy afternoons, she played Monopoly with her friends for hours before finally beating them all with only Boardwalk and Park Place. She didn't mind washing cars and washing the dog, but she'd never take a bath without a fight.

As a ten-year old, Saturday licked the brownie beaters, the cookie bowl, and the salt off her fingers. She squirted whipped cream directly into her mouth, or bit off the tip of the cone, sucking out the ice cream from the bottom. In summer, she picked a pail of blackberries without complaining about the bug bites, or filled a pail with sea shells that were still wet and sandy and smelled of the sea. At night, Saturday snuck her green beans to the dog under the dinner table and tipped back on the legs of her chair without anybody ever yelling about it. Saturday could always jump on the beds without getting caught.

Twelve-year-old Saturday played frenzied games of soccer, freeze tag, and foosball with her friends. Then she walked with them to 7-11 with only a couple of bucks in her pocket to buy a Slurpee or some candy cigarettes. If she had three dollars, she bought a ticket to the roller rink, hoping to share a Coke with the freckle-faced boy from math class. She never had much money, but she always shared with others.

Saturday was everybody's best friend.

When Saturday grew to be a teenager, she let her hair grow long and admired her new curves in the reflection of every shop window. She rode her motorcycle without a helmet or hung her arm out the car window and rode the wave with her hand in the breeze.

On weekends, she listened to her parent's old-timey music and danced while dusting the furniture. She'd have *one-on-one* time with her little sister, painting toenails on the back porch. Saturday could get her sister laughing so hard, she'd cry, hiccup and almost wet her pants.

Summer afternoons were for shelling peas in the shade with Grandma and not complaining about hearing the same family stories again and again. She'd have a water fight in the house with her best friend and her mom never found out. Their clothes would dry on their bodies in the summer heat.

Saturday always shared her popcorn at the movies. In

the evening, she ordered pizza with extra cheese, drank soda on the front porch with her friends, and never noticed when it got dark. Finally, she nestled down inside her sleeping bag, watching the stars and hoping the night would never end.

When Saturday grew up to be a woman, she wore ponytails and sneakers. She *slept in* because she could, even if she didn't really want to. She bought Slurpees at 7-11 and surprised her kids with them. Or she bought a Slurpee at 7-11, sat in the car, and drank it all by herself without telling anybody.

Saturday always ate off of paper plates.

If she was trying something new or taking a risk or being creative, Saturday would tuck her hair behind one ear and stick her tongue out just right.

While cleaning house, she opened the windows and danced along in the breeze with the flappy curtains.

At the movies, she didn't care that she looked like a cow whenever she ate popcorn. In the car, she didn't mind that she sang badly even if everyone else did.

Saturday spent hours playing cards on her daughter's bunk bed but never kept score. She gave all her *Draw-Twos* to the ones she loved best.

Saturday was friendly to the mailman or the ice cream vendor, even if she wasn't getting anything. She did the crossword puzzle with her feet up on the table and swam all afternoon, not worried about the sunburn she'd have later

When Saturday grew old, her hair thinned and her face shriveled, but her heart stayed like a young girl's. She sat in the sun until her hair felt hot; then played Ping-Pong downstairs in the basement with the freckle-faced boy from math class.

In the mornings, Saturday went for a walk without needing to get anywhere. She blew dandelion fluff and made a wish, or cheered loudly at the ball field full of kids she no longer recognized.

Saturday smelt like rain in the afternoon.

When Saturday died, her eulogy read:

*Saturday was freedom and happiness and simple pleasures, not to be traded for anything. Saturday was yesterday's memories and tomorrow's dreams. Saturday was pure and free and good and always said, Why not? or Let's try it! or Do it again! Her spirit will live on in our hearts, in our backyards, and on our funny faces. She will be missed.*

*There will be a receiving line at the door for anyone who wants to share their thoughts and condolences with Chase and Giggle and her husband, the freckle-faced boy from her math class.*

# Summer Storm

Hunched over his whittling stick on the front porch, Jeremy stilled his knife to listen to the whoosh of the refrigerator door. In the kitchen, his kid sister, Jemma, rummaged for the open package of hot dogs again. Today was Saturday. He'd let her eat the way she wanted to for now, but at suppertime, it would be cooked food, hot and good. Deli chicken and greens most likely. Something to sleep on. Something not too hard to fix.

Jeremy scraped another thin curl of white birch bark and stilled his knife again. Dangling at the end of the stick, the birch took its time to fall to the porch. He studied it and continued to listen.

The clinking of the bottles. The sucking sound of the refrigerator door as it closed. The slap of his sister's bare feet. The screen door hee-hawing behind her.

And then another sound that wasn't from inside the house—the crunch of gravel off in the distance. Car was coming down the road. Probably headed to the creek, what little bit of creek was left. It would be a while yet before Jeremy could make out the model. It was a long road.

Jeremy started up again with his knife at the top of the stick. He studied the slow glide of the blade against the white virgin wood, as if his knife was moving on its own, down the length of the stick. Another thin curl of birch dangled for the longest time before falling to the pile at his feet.

His sister loomed into view. Still sticky from breakfast, strands of uncombed hair stuck to her eight-year-old cheeks.

"Jemma." Jeremy's voice was low and sharp. He motioned for her to come nearer. "Watch yourself," he said and pointed to the pile of shavings.

Jemma raised her arms, a raw hot dog flopping in the tight grip of each little hand. She stepped over the pile to stand between her brother's long legs. Balancing the stick on one knee and the knife on the other, Jeremy held her head still while rubbing at the jelly on her cheeks with a worn handkerchief he kept folded in his pants pocket.

Her cut-off jeans were dirty, the tee shirt faded. Like those she had on, most of her clothes had been Jeremy's at one time. Those jeans had climbed trees with him, caught minnows at the creek, and chased fireflies with the dog. That was a lifetime ago, Jeremy thought, back when the summer sky promised rain. Back when his family was whole and right. Back when God was good.

Taking the hot dogs from her with distaste and balancing them on his legs along with the stick and knife, Jeremy went to work on her hands. Spitting into the handkerchief as needed, he hunched over the task in concentration and swiped at the sticky spots between each of her fingers.

As he worked, Jemma stared at Jeremy's furrowed face, cocking her head one way and then the other.

"Quit," he said.

"What?"

"Wiggling." But she didn't, and he didn't seem to mind enough to make her stop.

When he had done the best he could, he dropped her hands and looked at her face. The cloudless sky reflected in her brown eyes. The round cheeks were cleaner now than they'd been. The tiny mouth looked like a kitten's.

"I made up my mind about something," she said.

"Yeah?"

"You got the same face as Daddy."

Jeremy swallowed hard and gave a tight nod. He had developed his father's thick eyebrows. They had shared the same cowlick on one side. Sometime during the last school year, soft brown hair had sprouted on Jeremy's sharp chin and upper lip. His ears stuck out a bit like Daddy's and Big Daddy's, too. Only the thin scar above his left eye was unique to him alone, left long ago by one of Big Mama's cats. It was cause of that scar that Big Daddy never let the cats in the house again.

Jemma began to fidget. After a minute, she said, "Do I have anybody's face?" Hope tiptoed around in her words, but Jeremy couldn't bring himself to speak on it. He met her fixed gaze with silence until she tired of waiting and took back her two hot dogs.

Squatting down, she stirred his pile of wood shavings with one finger. At her touch, the slight breeze picked up some of the shavings and tumbled them across the porch. Jeremy watched them with patience. The only thing that ever seemed to be in a hurry around here was the wind.

He was about to pull out his stick again, and go to town whittling on it, when the car he had heard earlier drew near.

A brown Cadillac slowed and turned into Jeremy's driveway. The engine stopped and two men stepped out. Squinting against the sunlight, Jeremy saw they were wearing neckties and button-up shirts. Two women in dresses and fancy shoes climbed out of the backseat.

*Church folks,* Jeremy realized, and went back to his whittling.

✶✶✶✶✶✶✶✶✶✶✶✶✶

Five years ago, for his eighth birthday, Big Daddy gave Jeremy that pocket knife. For a whole week, Big Daddy showed his grandson's tender young fingers how to control the cuts. By applying the right pressure with his little thumb, he could carve wings on birds and faces on animals. Since then, Jeremy had rarely been without that knife, but he hadn't carved anything important in a long time. Whenever he'd close his eyes to think on it, no fish flapped around in his imagination; no bird flew by in his mind's eye. So he whittled toothpicks. He'd made two of them yesterday and kept them in his wallet.

That was the summer it rained every day for a month and the creek west of the house flooded her banks. Eight-year-old Jeremy took little Jemma down to the creek almost every day that summer. She was barely walking then, and she held tight to his thumbs as he led her over the smooth river rocks that composed their driveway. With their feet bare and their pants rolled up, he repeated tall tales his father had told him of talking gophers and friendly garter snakes until they reached the water's edge.

"Hold you," she whimpered when they'd come to the six inches of water flooded out onto the gravel drive.

"You'll be fine," he said, "it's just water." But when her toddler feet came out from under her just once, he caught her by the arm and scooped her up as best he could.

"See, I've got you. You're okay. It's just water, you're okay." When her brown eyes cleared up again, he set her down, making sure she wasn't wobbly. And then, there in the creek water that reached to her knees, Jeremy showed his sister how to catch minnows.

"If you don't talk or move, Jemma, you can catch a minnow," he'd say. "You gotta stand real still and hold your hand out real gentle." She was only three then and not much for keeping quiet or standing still. She never did catch a minnow that whole summer but he let her hold some of the ones he caught. They probably went to check on the minnows a dozen times or more before his schooling took up in the fall, but in the five years since, the creek had mostly dried up and they, neither one, had been back.

That was the summer Big Daddy built the roof over the carport. The rain, wind, and sun had done their best work against that old dirt driveway, leaving it packed, rutted and muddy most of the time. Big Mama dreaded getting in and out of the Lincoln in her church shoes for fear of twisting her ankle in the mud.

After choosing to stay home from church two weeks in a row and worrying Big Daddy about the condition of their souls night and day, he'd finally had enough of her henpecking. Without a word, he stood up straight, all six-foot-seven of him, threw down the evening paper and marched out of the house, leaving his wife and dog to look and wonder what had gotten into him.

Grabbing his old blackened John Deere hat and keys, hanging outside the back door, Big Daddy stomped out to his truck in the rain. From the front window, Jeremy could see him slipping in the mud and nearly falling backwards a few times. Daddy followed after him, arms overhead, poorly protected against the wet.

When Big Daddy backed up right over her flower beds, Jeremy and Big Mama saw it all. She let out a shriek and Big Daddy threw his head back and cackled as he drove away down the lane.

By the time the rain stopped an hour later, Jeremy heard the clunking and bumping of the truck coming up the drive. The bed was loaded up with two by fours, wooden planks and sheet metal. It looked like someone had taken apart an old chicken coop, piece by piece, and stacked it up in the truck bed.

"Help us unload all this, boy." When his grandfather called him *boy*, it was never in a mean way, not like other men folk from town who'd sneer and put you down as soon as look at you, just for wearing second-hand clothes or what-have-you. Jeremy reached out for a bucket of nails and the old hammer.

When the supplies were unloaded and stacked by the back door, Big Daddy hung the keys on the nail and placed his John Deere cap back over it. He stopped at the sink to get a drink of water and strode by Big Mama on the way to the bedroom.

"First thing in the morning," he said, "it'll be done."

That sheet metal roofing was up by noon, and Jeremy helped Daddy and Big Daddy fill in the driveway and rake it smooth before supper. When Big Daddy came in, he grabbed Big Mama's face with his dirt-caked, calloused hands, kissed her soundly on the cheek, and said, "Done and done."

*************

"Morning, boy," called the man who'd been driving the big car. "Jeremy, isn't it?" As if on cue, the whole gaggle of them stepped closer to the porch, approaching the children carefully as if they might startle and run away.

"Sir," Jeremy said, his voice low and his body rigid like a cornered dog's.

The last time the church had sent folks out was when Mama and Daddy died. It was that same summer; the rain fell in sheets most afternoons and evenings. Sheriff said they probably couldn't see the road. It was a hit and run—most likely a drunk driver.

Church folks came by in their nice cars and neckties. They brought covered dishes and offered to help around the house, but after being underfoot for a week or two, Big Daddy told them to go on, said they'd get by.

"The Good Lord's got His ways and I got mine," Big Daddy said. "I don't blame Him. What comes, comes." He watched them drive away, back down the long road to town. They didn't come by their place after that except to wave as they headed toward the mouth of the creek for a baptism.

In the months that followed, the carport rusted and cracked. The grass grew and the rain stopped. Big Daddy never did get over losing his son that way. He wasn't much use for anything after that—not for working or praying or consoling the grandkids.

Big Mama couldn't do anything with him either so she gave up trying and crawled into bed. It seemed to Jeremy that she just gave up—her bird feeders, her flower beds. She still got up to feed the cats. It was the only thing she did do, and since the Lincoln was totaled in the accident, those nasty cats took up residence under the carport.

Big Daddy laid up in his recliner, nursing his morning coffee from sunup till after the six o'clock news, so there wasn't much use in Jeremy's trying to fend them off. At first it was just the carport—always smelling like mildew and cat piss, but when Big Mama started letting them back in the house—from then on, Jeremy spent the better part of each day out on the porch or fiddling in the shed, away from the stink of the cats.

The sun ducked behind a cloud. A slight breeze troubled the trees against the graying sky. Jeremy stopped squinting and just stared at the four strangers, who stared back. The women wore wobbly smiles.

Jemma climbed down from where she'd been walking heel-to-toe on the porch rail and hovered bashfully behind her brother, clutching at his leg and peeking out from behind his jeans.

"Your grandparents around? We've come for a visit."

"They're both home." Jeremy remained guarded. "Not much up for visiting folks though."

The woman in the blue dress stepped closer. Her brown hair was twisted up and her voice came out too soft, like she was sweet-talking a baby.

"My, you've gotten tall, Jeremy. Why, I remember you being in my Sunday school some years ago. Do you remember me, honey—Miss Cummings?"

"Ma'am," Jeremy acknowledged with a slight nod.

She grinned and clutched her purse in front of her like she thought a bird might swoop down to take it.

"And who's this pretty little thing?" the lady in the white blouse said, eyeing Jemma with her twinkly, crinkly eyes. "What's your name, sweetheart?"

"This is Jemma," Jeremy said. "She's eight."

The older man came right up to the steps. "Would it be okay if we came up to visit with you for a bit?" he asked. "Maybe your grandfather will come out directly and talk a spell."

"Yessir," Jeremy said.

There were only four chairs on the porch, and he really didn't want to do anything to encourage them to stay longer, but for politeness' sake, he stepped into the house to grab two kitchen chairs.

Walking in, Jeremy found the house was quiet and dark. Getting a whiff of Big Mama's cats nearly turned his stomach. He would be relieved once eighth grade started in the fall and he'd be away from here most of the day.

"Folks from the church come for a visit," he called into the quietness of the house. Jeremy didn't know what he expected anybody to do about it—he certainly didn't feel like entertaining folks—but he didn't want to get scolded for not letting a body know either. The TV was quiet in the other room. There was no creak of any kind, no movement. It was as if the house itself held its breath to see what Jeremy would do.

"I'll be out front if you need me," he offered weakly to the dark, empty front room.

Jeremy managed to get the two kitchen chairs through the door without assistance. The screen door banged into place. Somewhere back toward town, the darkening sky echoed with distant thunder. The women had arranged themselves on the porch chairs and were trying to coax Jemma into talking or sitting on their laps.

The men took the two kitchen chairs and settled themselves in a half circle in front of the others. Jeremy sat down reluctantly. If he didn't offer them a cold drink, they might get on their way. He wasn't sure what they come for or what they were going to say, but he didn't think he was going to care much for it either way.

The driver leaned back in his chair and propped one ankle on his knee. He seemed to study Jeremy as he spoke, "It's quite a dry spell we've been having."

"Yessir."

The older man looked at the driver and cleared his throat. "I'm sorry, boy, about your folks," he stammered. "I knew your dad real well. He was a fine man."

A shiver swept through Jeremy's back and shoulders and crawled up his neck to roost in his head. He took a steadying breath. Jemma clambered over to him and scooted in to sit on the chair alongside him.

With difficulty, Jeremy met the man's eyes.

"Yessir." He didn't want to look around at the others for fear of seeing pity in their faces. Or something else.

The older man spoke up again. "We've missed you at church, son—you and your family."

One day Big Daddy stopped bringing them to church altogether. Jeremy and God didn't talk much after that. He tried to keep his feelings about God straight in his head but it wasn't pressing on him. He guessed the day would come when he'd have to make up his mind about God, but he wasn't sure he wanted it to be today.

"I hoped," the man went on, "I wondered…" Jeremy looked down at the pile of wood shavings still lying on the porch at his feet. The sky was darkening and threatening to rain. He'd have to sweep that pile up before it got wet and made a mess of Big Mama's porch.

"I'm sorry for your loss, and we would like to be of help. We are your church family, after all. We…"

*Family?* Jeremy thought. *It's been five years, where have you been?* He opened his mouth and closed it again.

"I know you may not feel like it, Jeremy…" This time

the driver spoke. He looked to the older man as if he expected to be challenged. He placed his hand on the boy's knee. Jeremy peered down at it, like it would burn a hole into his leg, as he heard the man say, "…but God still loves you, even if you don't come to church anymore."

Jeremy's mouth went dry. His face was hot. His head felt fuzzy. Something like a glowing coal seemed to let loose and crackle inside his brain. He studied the uneven planks of the porch beneath the chairs where the two men sat. His heart beat against his chest. When he glanced up into the man's face, he spoke in a low, sharp growl.

"Jemma. Get in the house."

She hesitated and he pushed her off the chair. Grabbing her shoulders a little more roughly than before, Jeremy directed her around the pile of shavings. The sky crackled as she protested. Never taking his eyes off the man, he listened for the screen door to slam behind her.

The scar above his eye began to throb. He managed to keep his voice low, his words deliberate.

"God still loves me?" Jeremy's voice cracked and he looked back and forth at the women, who were fidgeting with their purses and earrings. He scooted up a little in his chair and clutched his hands in front of him, rubbing them up and down his pant legs. His head was spinning.

"God still loves me, even if he killed off my parents and ruined everything for everybody?" Jeremy choked on his emotion and began coughing. A few scattered drops of rain fell in his hair and on his arm. It made him flinch.

"God's not like that, boy," the older man said. The sky grew darker.

"I don't want to know what God is like."

Jeremy felt so hot, despite the rain. Something like a rock wedged itself into his throat, making it hard to speak. His words came out in a squeak, "What am I supposed to say when Jemma asks me about God and Mama and Daddy and every other stupid question in the world—I got no answers for her. I got nothing."

He grabbed his head to keep it from spinning. One of the women started weeping softly but Jeremy didn't look up to see which one.

"Boy," the driver said, but not the way Big Daddy always said it, "you better watch yourself."

Jeremy raked his eyes over the man who sat across from him looking like he was itching for a fight. Rain fell a little heavier now. Water dripped into the man's face but he held Jeremy's gaze.

From the corner of his eye, Jeremy could see lightning flash and, several seconds later, thunder boomed.

The women started to squirm is if to plead, *It's time to get out of here.*

Then something else boomed and the screen door hee-hawed on its hinges.

"Get on outta here!"

Jeremy felt Big Daddy grow larger than life behind him as he spoke again, "I ain't about to listen to any of y'all beat up on this boy with all your church talk."

Forgetting propriety, the women gasped and hurdled toward the stairs, their purses held over their heads. The driver cleared his throat and with a nod to Big Daddy, headed back to the car like a whipped pup. Jeremy followed them with his eyes but none of them ever looked back.

Big Daddy turned to the older man, still brave enough to stay put. "Grant."

"Jim."

"You best be getting on with the rest of them."

"I didn't mean no harm, Jim. I'm sorry." The older man loped down the stairs, climbed in the car and the whole lot of them backed up, careful not to drive up into the grass. They drove on back down the long road to town, out of spitting distance and out of sight.

The rain was falling so hard, Jeremy couldn't make

out Big Daddy's face, but there was no mistaking that authority had returned to his low voice as he took Jeremy by the shoulders and spoke.

"Jeremy, I know my God, and I don't blame Him. I'm not afraid. He lost His Son, too—He knows what we're feeling."

Rain was in his eyes, in his ears and he was soaked from top to bottom, but Jeremy listened to Big Daddy without interrupting. It was the most he had heard him speak in five years.

"Now, come in the house, boy."

Thunder boomed on down the road and the rain slowed. Big Daddy held the screen door open, and Big Mama was waiting inside with a bundle of clean towels.

Jeremy was grateful to wipe his face and dry his hair a little, but he wasn't ready to get dry clothes on just yet.

"Big Mama," Jeremy said as tenderly as he could, "this carpet stinks. I just can't take it anymore. It's got to go."

Big Mama started to protest, but Big Daddy stared her down and handed her his towel. "I think the rain's letting up. Let's get this recliner outta here."

With a whimper, Big Mama picked up her rocker and hobbled it into the doorway of Jemma's room.

Big Daddy hollered from the living room, "It's just a

rug, woman, let it go."

Jeremy caught Jemma's eye and smiled a little. She crawled up in Big Mama's lap and they rocked together, watching and listening to the men rumble through the house like a summer storm.

When a corner became cleared of furniture, Jeremy yanked that first section of carpet up from the floor to expose a beautiful wood floor beneath it. Digging down into his pocket, he gripped his faithful pocket knife and started going to town on that nasty cat-piss carpet, cutting it into squares and throwing them in a pile near the screen door. With every yank, every cutting, something let loose inside Jeremy, too.

The sky cleared up, a mournful shade of blue peeking through the trees.

That night after Big Daddy tucked Jemma into bed with a whiskered-kiss to the forehead, he poked his head into Jeremy's room

"Boy," Big Daddy said as he turned off his light, "tomorrow we'll start sanding and staining that floor in there.

"Yessir."

"But first thing before that, we're gonna get them cats outta here."

Before going to sleep Jeremy snuck over to Jemma's room and sat on the edge of her bed. "You know, Jem, I been thinking."

"Yeah?" she slurred sleepily.

"I think you got Mama's eyes."

"Really?"

"Yeah, really." Then he kissed the top of her head and went back to bed.

Made in the
USA
Middletown, DE